I0679913

Lady Alpha

Absolute Unit, Volume 1

E.L. Southwick

Published by Cindrebooks, 2024.

This is a work of fiction. Similarities to real people, places, or events are entirely coincidental.

LADY ALPHA

First edition. August 19, 2024.

ISBN: 979-8999381910

Written by E.L. Southwick.

Table of Contents

To MTP and the people we were

Chapter 1 - Alpha

The short dress, a clingy wine-red mini with a deep plunge and a halter neck that I bought specially to match this lipstick, might be making it *too* easy for strong hands sliding their way up my thighs. We are pressed together in the dark space next to a wall, next to a pillar. He will make a case that it's a defense tactic to have me in a corner; I know he just likes to pin me back so he can get better access. I'm off balance, tip toeing in my heels, but it doesn't matter. My Beta has me. My free hand is clasped on the back of his neck, disrupting his curls and his cologne. His desperate mouth is against mine, nibbling my neck, kissing his way up my chin. I glanced idly around the dark room, but my body is responding like always. I can't help but push against him. Every part of me wants to drag him out to the truck and hop on his lap. He knows my little undertones of *desperate* want.

Everyone here knows who I am. They can feel it. They've seen me in daylight, and Ash under the moon. There's gawkers. There's the forward ones carefully waiting to get my attention. There are wary ones skulking the edges.

Across the room, my Delta observes the bar games, flicking his gaze over to the dance floor, and then flashing an eye my way, swigging from a beer bottle in between. In a hushed tone, the redhead wrapped solidly under his shoulder with her fingertips on his chest sips her own drink, whispering to him. Delta is softly menacing - he is holding himself rigidly, issuing an open invitation to troublemakers to try their luck, but when he turns back every few seconds to my second Beta, the corners of his eyes crinkle. He relaxes an iota, but only with her coaxing.

The atmosphere changes as my Gamma comes back into the room. Beta keeps his face turned to my neck, but pulls back his grazing teeth with a searing kiss.

What is it? I ask through the mindlink, open to my staff. I'm not looking at them; I'm nuzzling Beta's shoulder. He hides his sigh of irritation, moving one hand from my waist to the wall behind my back.

This place is older than it looks. Gamma has no game face. He is trying to look casual, sidling next to Delta and Beta across the room, but his eyes are wide and worried. Delta looks like he is coughing, all of a sudden, and takes a step away.

So? I ran my lacquered nails down the smooth cloth of Beta's shirt, shoulder to hip.

There's a ladder down to some backrooms. I swear to you Alpha, there's Omegas down there, and they don't smell of Glacier Moon.

Over Beta's shoulder, I have a good view of the bar at the back, and the owner looking back at me. I'm sure his business registration says bar and lounge, and not brothel, and even if it did, everyone here *knows* me.

Everyone here knows how we deal with Omegas. Inner wolf Ash expresses her confusion.

I reluctantly pull my hand from behind Beta's neck, as he looks down at me between his arms. He plucked the cherry out of his Old Fashioned, impaled on a tiny neon sword, and offered it to me, waiting for the silent nod.

The four of them separate like a thunderclap, leaving me to observe, arms crossed, in the shadowy corner by the pillar. The lights fly up and the music skids to a halt. From the bar, the owner is hurriedly working on a shotgun, glancing up to locate me.

Always, every time we go out, there's drama, Second Beta sighs, ushering the patrons out into the icy night. She's also wearing a short, ruched dress and ankle boots so they don't take her seriously right away, and her mate, my Delta, is pacing and snarling as a result. We can see, Ash and I, that he is torn between targets. Does he knock some heads on behalf of the Beta, or does he flay the man threatening his Alpha?

Logic would dictate that the consistent feature is me, that I'm creating the drama, but I disagree. Not that I don't welcome the change of pace. *Alpha* is a title with no work life balance. The pressure can be consuming, physically crushing, but also monotonous, so the *occasional* spark of drama is entertaining. But sometimes, downright depressing, the amount of people I have to murder in one night.

The work of changing minds takes decades, I mused to the wolf, ducking a thrown bottle in the bar area. *'Let's get out of the Central for once,'* my Beta had begged, *'Let's go to the Northward and see how they are doing.'* He sure regretted that now.

He didn't know, sighed Ash, who always takes Cole's side anyway.

Work, work, work, it's always work. With a few persuasive snaps of her teeth, my second Beta had cleared the club, while my Gamma was in the basement documenting the violations that were about to get this guy jailed if he was lucky, and murdered if he didn't put the shotgun down in the next 10 seconds. Beta and Delta were quickly pinching in from either side, with me down the center.

"It's loaded with silver," the owner said ominously, keeping it aimed at me. I rolled my eyes.

For that reason alone, I could kill this guy. It's one thing to keep a gun here - they are almost totally useless and the folks who insist on them are normally shifters who were not raised in the Packlands. They retain weird human hang ups. Even if he had a full club riot on his hands, a gun would only guarantee a slippery floor.

Throwing a squeaky toy would be better crowd control.

But a gun loaded with silver? That's a clear felony, in my eyes *and* the eyes of the Pack laws.

Which are conveniently the same thing! Ash is ready to pounce.

"I don't know why you came back here," I said slowly, giving my officers time to get into position.

Any compelling reason not to pop his head off like a grape? Easton asked me through the mind link.

I wanna chew his face off myself! Ash answers, although Easton can't hear her.

Ew, I don't. He looks gristly. The mental image makes me gag.

"Did you expect me to not find out what you were doing?" I continue. My parents banished this asshole years ago. That represented mercy, but no more.

He conveniently returns when the reins of power change, thinks he can sniff out an opportunity? Thing is, I might have allowed him to return. I might have allowed him to run a bar. God knows, I love a change of scene, and dance music the louder the better.

If I do say so, I'm great for business!

But not like this. Not back to these dirty old ways. I trust my Beta and my Gamma and my own ears and nose. I know what he's got in the basement.

Make him drop it, Ash suggests.

He's not worth the energy, I retort, slowly advancing.

"Laws are different where I came from."

No begging, no I'm so sorry my Alpha, no promises to reform. Not good enough, Barkeep my good sir!

DO IT! She whines in my head, *MAKE THE VOICE!*

"No," I answer him, with a head toss.

The nerve!

Slavery has been outlawed for literal decades, since before my parents were even born. We don't keep the Omegas as slaves, or even servants if we can help it. I have exhausted myself, on top of all of my other work and responsibilities, with removing the Omega mark from any wolf that asks. Sure, of course shifter wolves are smarter and better than your basic humans, but there is still an intrinsic social classism that I find gross. I can't stop all the Omegas from being mistreated, but little by little, we are changing cultural norms.

I am close enough now to touch the barrel of the shotgun if I leapt forward. He is aiming down quite a bit, since I am on the short side even with dance club heels.

"Maybe you should go back to where you came from?" suggests Beta Cole, where he is just behind this asshole now. With a sideways look of surprise - no one can out stealth my mate- the gun swings out of my face. A crunch of shattering bone and ruptured organs tells the whole story. Easton and Cole stand with the remains of the big male shredded on the floor between them, while I am on tiptoe, leaning over the bar, holding the gun by the barrel in the air where he left it.

While as an individual he gets on my every last damn nerve, say what you want, Easton is a competent Delta. Super strong and *super* impatient. He's not waiting for the Gamma to philosophize about events. He's not rationalizing anything. He's here to let nature take its course, and on that, he and I agree. Still, he would just be another washed up high school soccer player if it weren't for his wife. He's much more brawn than brain, let's say, which is about par for a Delta, but still not my preference. I'm *trying* to be progressive; disembowel first, ask questions later, is not always compatible.

His wife is very convincing though!

I nod to Easton and he swiftly takes the gun from me and unloads it, dropping the silver shells onto the bar.

Is it me, or is Eazy more agitated than usual?

Maybe check him for fleas? Ash is a sass.

Cole kicks the bloody mess on the floor out of the way, knocking bottles over to sweep for the rest of the ammunition that he *expects* to find under the bar.

"I don't even know why you pay a security force," Easton drawls with disdain, as they both dig out a sloppily hidden trove of various substances and weapons. Easton rinses the sinews and bone shards from his exposed claws with a cracked bottle of grain alcohol before retracting them.

Maybe he was just feeling unclean, and that's why he is so twitchy?

*You should demote **him** to security*, Ash mutters to me.

"Can't call them now," Cole meets my eyes with an eyebrow lift. He's right. I'll have to call my own trusted team from the central locale. It's entirely likely that the security team up here in Northward have been paid off or employed by this asshole.

So. Many. Murders.

Justice revisions, Ash says smugly, leaping about in my head. If ADHD had a face, it was this wolf.

Chapter 2- Omega Rescue

U*m, there is blood dripping down the back wall of this dungeon*, says Grant, my sturdy Gamma, *Everything ok?*

Not ours, I respond.

Got it.

How many down there?

Five. Four female and one male.

I wince and Cole looks at me with concern. His wolf and mine communicate with their own connection; I know Ash passes all my thoughts to him. And I can see, knowing him as long as I have, that Falcon is fighting him to leap over this bar and lick me all over, to reassure himself that I am fine, and to soothe my elevated anxiety. But I am the Alpha and he may not approach me without leave. I mean, he *may not* but certainly *has* before; it's not like Ash would actually stop him.

He's trying to be respectful.

In a minute. There's still work to do.

It's not their fault they're Omegas, Ash reminds me.

I know, I don't blame them. Deeply enslaved Omegas need a lot of support. The body keeps the score and that lifelong abuse has persistent flare ups. I have directed my Pack, both as a group and as individuals, to provide that help, but it can be a big ask for both parties. Wolves are not naturally disposed to kindness towards weak members. The oppressed are not great at using their words.

But we are more than wolves.

We are greater than humans.

We are having a lot of visitors, Beta Brooke sends us from the front, where she is maintaining the periphery.

You ok? Easton snarls, kicking a suspicious plastic tub as he jumps over the counter, bullets and debris rolling out of his way. He stands beside me, tacitly asking permission to go downstairs to his mate. There's a hint of defiance, like I better be granting that permission with *speed*. I know where his loyalty lies.

Mmm Hmm, Brooke answers with distraction. Easton grunts beside me. Cole has come back around the counter now as well. There is an array of obnoxious substances and weapons laid out behind us.

"Alpha, I need to get out of this room," Easton is waiting, tethered to me but edgy.

"This'll keep." Cole's voice is quiet, "Let's go see what Brookey's looking at and what shape the Omegas are in."

Any Lycans down there? I ask Grant. They may be the "Ruling Class" but their ability to be enslaved as children is truly baffling. And they can be hard to suss out until they come of age and just destroy the shit out of everything.

Well..... He sighs.

Great.

"New friends!" Ash is basically doing flips in the air. She is the least Alpha wolf ever. And honestly, that's the only reason I've managed, the only reason I could accept the position. She is a joy and an unbridled delight.

I was never supposed to be the Alpha. But things happen.

Back at the Packhouse, the Luna, my twin sister, is waiting on the steps with her officers. Not for the first time, I contrast her dark features with my lighter ones. She is the one swathed in dignity. She would have fit the Alpha role better, but she couldn't because she is not a wolf shifter. So, she has to make do with the secondary role, but Queenship suites her. She got the Naiad side, like all my siblings, and favors my mother with silky dark hair and dark eyes. I went after my father's side, I assume, with unruly shoulder length blonde hair and blue eyes.

My dad married for...maybe love, if you choose to believe that a person can have more than one love in their lives. Power. Safety. A permanent inclination towards mischief that he has not always been able to control. But my mother never hid what she was - a water shifter, a wispy being that prowls in the shadows of deep pools and drags down the unwary and dishonest. At least, that's what she's reverted to since the divorce. The populace of our Pack, the Glacier Moon Pack, have always had a healthy respect for her, honored her as Luna, maybe crossed the street in deference when they saw her coming. But to me, she was just mom, who made pancakes and blew up balloons for birthdays and posed us for family holiday cards in matching long johns with ass flaps. She pops up now and then, usually with no warning.

In the years since the divorce, one by one, my siblings came of age. Ellie, my oldest sister, turned out to be Naiad, and went on to run the Pack hospital. She says she always knew, even when she was dutifully following my parents around and preparing for the leadership role that never came. The former Alpha, my father, will never admit it, but my older brother

Joshi is so much like him, even down to some of the natural ice talents that run in my father's family line. Joshi being wolfless was a major blow. Plus, dad's marriage was on the rocks, he was plagued with self doubt as he had met someone else, and he would have liked to pass on the Alpha role at that time. Joshi would have accepted, begrudgingly, but he's not super social and it would have been a burden. Even at the best of times, it can be a burden. But then he, and all of them, had to *wait* until Violet and I turned 21, because Joshi also turned out to be a Naiad.

Two years we waited, and it's been two years since my twin and I were thrust into these roles. Roles we never assumed for ourselves - why would we? We had two older siblings. At best, we would leave the territory as Luna to some other Pack. Well, *Violet* would have. I made sure, when I was 16, that I was never leaving the lands and people that I love.

Now, I nod to my sister, gesturing to the five Omegas we pulled out of the basement. They look awful, of course, because they are kept half starved and weak. This has never made any sense to me.

Where are you? I demand of Easton and Brooke, who were in the other vehicle. Easton usually drives like we are filming a chase scene. I expected them to beat us. There is something off about him tonight that I can't quite identify.

Coming down the drive now. I can hear the hesitation in Brooke's voice. Something to ask about when I see her.

But the Omegas. I don't know why some wolves are born into this class. As you can guess by the fact that my mother is a minor deity, we don't exactly ascribe to the Church of the Moon Goddess, Lunar Rites, like most other shifter wolves.

There are a lot of holes in Moon Goddess doctrine that don't make sense, slavery least of all. Why enslave something that can't escape; where are the Omegas going to go? They aren't as athletic as the other classes of wolf. Even if they are in service jobs *by choice*, how are they supposed to perform all their tasks if they are half dead? How can it possibly be no trouble to schedule in time for beatings, but far too much bother to just feed them regular meals? If you are really feeling cheap, tell them to *shift* and send them out after voles or something. Ash loves when she catches her own meat, it's her favorite day. It's not that hard at all to treat others with basic acknowledgement. And don't even get me started on Fated Mates and Omegas!

Luna Violet is calming and gracious, welcoming the slaves into the warm glow of the Packhouse. She has an office dedicated to Omega management. There are foster families and medical evaluations and remedial school and self defense classes in their future. Good amount of therapy and therapeutic running around in the clean, biting snow. The Lycan, the only male in the group, is gonna be a real problem. Violet and I exchange glances as he files past her into the house. He's surely an orphaned heir, they always are, and that means someone is looking for him. He's the second one we've picked up since we started getting aggressive about trafficking, and the last one was a real ordeal. But I did make some helpful contacts.

We'll hear him out tomorrow.

It's tomorrow now, Ash points out.

Later tomorrow. Right now, I need a swim. I gotta get the crusty blood off my body.

Chapter 3 – Glacier Moon Dynamics

Yay! Ash does a joyful prance. She still hasn't figured out swim means shower. She will tolerate a shower if I don't make a big deal out of it. I tried to take a bath once after my first shift and that did not go well so we don't say the 'bath' word in the house anymore. Just to be a confounding nuisance, she will completely take over my body to leap into any natural pool of water with pure canine delight. Ever since my mom got kinda feral, we are the only ones who do, so it's a great way to get away from Pack problems.

Sniff our babies first! Ash demands.

Cole is already checking on them. She's also not a baby anymore; she turned 8 last winter. The twin boys are 3.

Mine! MINE! There is no arguing with her. She will never let me get through a shower if I don't let her check on my children first. She wasn't even around when I was pregnant with them, but it took Ash *zero* minutes to realize that I had found, mated, and marked Cole without any of her help years before she appeared. If she was disappointed that she didn't get to guide that process, as most wolves do, she wasted no time dwelling.

The concept of twins did give her pause. She was a devoted fan of Cole and his wolf Falcon from the second she gained consciousness. But why then, was there a female who closely resembled Cole, smelled remarkably like him?

Also, question? She had ventured, sniffing aggressively, leaving scorch marks in the floor before we learned to be more careful, *This dark haired girl, more than sister? Does not smell like other sister. What is this thing?*

Do you mean twin? Violet is my twin. Brookey is Cole's twin. Twin is...?

The babies are twins. It's kind of common at Glacier Moon. She had been bouncing around, sniffing everything emphatically, but she paused to think.

Hm. Where is our Autumn's twin?

Thankfully, she was a singleton. The boys were bad enough. If I'd had twins with my first pregnancy, no chance I'd have let Cole touch me again. Autumn came easily, and before I knew it, suddenly I was twice as big and there were two heartbeats on the monitor screen.

Hm. I smell everything. This guy here smells like whiskey mouthwash, and mud grass!

Ash regarded Easton with narrowed eyes. She liked him even less when he doused the smoldering wood around her paws with water and ushered her outdoors into the snow.

I can smell vanilla, now. There's blood and entrails, dungeon must, and a chemical chaser from the cheap alcohol and various substances, but underneath, Cole smells like a birthday cake in the oven. We meet up in the hallway, and I poke my face into our daughter's bedroom so that Ash will settle.

"Swim?" he asks, ruefully, as I reach over to pull something grossly intestinal out of his hair.

"Yes!" He takes my hand and we turn into the next doorway off the hall.

Once clean, I'm throwing tasks off my to-do list. I am not up for a dawn run. I am up for breakfast and then I've got to make some kind of determination over the Northward security force. I'm not having traitors terrorizing my citizens, or running their own unregulated side business in underage Omegas and drugs. The Lycan I'll leave for later. The second he's strong enough, and I remove the Omega designation from him, whoever is looking for him will be able to sense him and we will be swarmed by Lycans and anyone who wants a chance at a crown. They are conceited and pushy, but hopefully learned some good lessons last time.

Yes, this is an odd Pack where the Luna is a Naiad *and* the Luna is my sister. Yes, I have two Betas, they are twin siblings, and I'm mated to one of them. My dad divorced a vengeful goddess, and abdicated the Alpha role so he could live his truth with a lovely, mousy man who writes unprintably raunchy werewolf romances. Yes, I am a female, *and* the Alpha, and was never in line for *any* of this shit. And yes, per my father, a well known rebel. An unrepentant teen mom. And something else altogether, something that gives even Lycans a flash of respect. In this land of winter, over the backdrop of icy spines, I have fire in my fingers.

It's never been seen in my family before. My mother comes from water dwelling people, and the Alphas on my father's side have been gifted manipulation over ice and snow. My sisters got the water gifts, and my brother is like my dad. But not me. I can snap my fingers and draw down a flame into my hand, a gift that came with Ash. I've dealt some lasting lessons to other

Pack leaders who come to Glacier Moon looking to expand their territory or consolidate their power.

It's too early for even the early shift of breakfast, but there's no point to sleeping. Ash disagrees; she is snoozing.

No point to sleeping! Meet in the kitchen. I order my staff. My Beta rolls his eyes with a smirk as he buttons up a flannel shirt.

"I'll make you some bacon," I promise him.

"That's not what I was hoping for," he winks, doing a little hop as he pulls on socks. I was about to demand some clarification, but there's no time for nakeds this morning.

Really? Comes a breathy whine from his sister, *I was just getting to the good part.*

GROSS!

In my dream! I was ASLEEP!

There's work to do. Sleep later.

Oohhhhhkaaaaaay....

You too, Grant!

Oh, I went out for the morning run, I'll meet you in the kitchen.

Chapter 4 – Ethics

Within a few minutes, Cole had wolfy sized portions of bacon and toast going and we were all on barstools around the island countertop. Grant sauntered in carrying his boots, wrapping a towel around his waist.

"I'll go with you next time," Easton said, "I need to get out of this house."

Brooke pouted, "I don't like early mornings."

"This is really still last night," Grant pointed out.

"All I wanted was to go dancing," I said darkly into my coffee.

"I know," Brooke said, "You just can't help it, wherever you go: drama. They wait until they sense you coming."

"I'm so over it. And now we have to ...*manage*...the whole north territory security team? Then what? The team here is depleted."

"I'll go up and organize a transitional security force, if you like," Easton said quietly, holding a coffee mug up to his mouth. Brooke and I both stared at him.

"Ok, and what the hell am I supposed to do without a Delta here, when all the Lycans show up for the kid in the basement?"

Easton put his free hand up, still holding his coffee, "I meant, like, for a day or two. Like I could go up there today and be back tomorrow. Send around a sign up for a border patrol, that's it."

Brooke blinked at him, with her eyebrows raised.

"What? Pack security is my thing and right now, that's our weak point. You mentioned Lycans. They don't always use the gates."

"Well hopefully *some* of them are innocent." Grant dipped his toast into an egg.

I sighed, twirling my bacon.

"Violet is the best lie detector, although I feel bad to be putting another task on her already overfull day."

There was something intrinsic to Naiads - they could feel the vibrations of sincerity in your breath and in your words. The Glacier Moon Luna was not to be trifled with.

"How about your mother? She's been around lately, lurking under the shrine bridge?"

Have you ever looked over a bridge to the dark water underneath? That's not your face looking back at you.

I consider this, "If we just throw them into the pond, that could be more efficient. She can judge them. Saves time having to murder them all later."

Grant coughed.

"Sorry, having to 'dispense justice.'" I looked over my officers as I drummed my fingers on the white marble bar. We looked tired, but there would be time to sleep later. Easton sat with his eyes closed, holding the mug in both hands in front of his face.

"Do you need some more coffee?" I asked him, doubtfully. Brooke looked over to her mate, knitting her red eyebrows together.

"What, me? No." He smiled, pushing back from the counter. He reached out an arm for Brooke and pulled her in, burying his face in her neck for a moment, kissing her cheek as he resurfaced. "What's next? Are we serving breakfast to the condemned or keeping the budget in mind and booting them into the pond at first light?"

Brooke seemed to have some deeper level of tether in the Pack mindlink. Her and Cole's father, Gabe, was the former Delta. Pretty much the only thing that saved Easton from the ass kicking of his life when Brooke was caught sneaking out to meet him was that Easton was already lined up to be my brother's Delta, *had* Joshi been a wolf shifter.

So, while Cole and Grant debated whether sausages were only for *good* wolfies who did *not* traffic in slavery versus international standards on criminal rights, I noticed that Brooke's demeanor was a little stiff next to her mate. There was appraisal in her eyes as she looked him over quietly. And just for a flicker of a moment, I saw her wolf, Persia, slide over her features. Something was definitely going on with this couple.

"Should we go out to the pond?" Cole asked me, rinsing out a pan and drying his hands. The morning crew would be in at any minute to lay out the daily house breakfast.

Ash, I prodded, *Ask Falcon if he knows what's up with Persia?"*

What is wrong with Persia? Ash asks me lazily.

Is she fighting with Roust for some reason?

How about - more bacon?

How about - you answer my question? No more bacon now; I've gotta wrestle some accused security into a -

Into a what?

Into a swim. So they can meet my mother.

Oh, so she can drown them. Clever. Ash agrees, *Here comes our baby!*

Autumn kicked open the kitchen door, fetched a bowl and some cereal and climbed up a barstool beside us.

"Morning," chorused the crew. Brooke stepped away from her mate, fetching the milk from the fridge. Easton smiled indulgently at my daughter - he had, after all, spent a lot of 'study nights' babysitting her for the years that Brookey and Cole were restricted to the Delta apartment. And then he said, "I'm gonna go outside and see if the pond is frozen, maybe chop a hole in the ice if needed."

I thought about calling him back, because as he well knew, I would just melt the surface in a moment, but this gave me an opening with Brooke so let him run around in the snow like a puppy.

Whatever.

"This looks bright," I said to Autumn, examining her cereal. The breakfast shift came in, everything got busy, we spent a few minutes with our daughter, and our twins as they came in as well, and then I headed out to the main dining room to find the Luna.

"Everything ok?" I murmured to Brooke in the hallway. I'm not going to give her a chance to deny it. "He's weird and it's making you quiet. What is going on?"

"I think he hurt himself," Brooke answered, "Back at Northward. He was actually slow to get to the truck and he drove much slower than usual."

If he's injured, I didn't see it.

Or smell it.

But what I did see and smell was a rack ton of illegal substances, and what I'm wondering now is if my Delta has a drug problem.

"Ok," I answer, hiding my doubt, "But if he's not fully healed by tonight then he's gotta get checked out. Something wrong with *Roust* that it's taking longer than usual?" Again, I see Persia flash across her features.

"We already had a full schedule before you brought in four Omegas, a Lycan, and some sketchy security officers," Violet drawls, interrupting us. "Where do you wanna start? Hard stop at 3:30 because we have the union negotiation meeting. There's lawyers involved and they cost money. I moved everything else for you."

Hard stop at 12 for a nap. Cole sends from behind me.

"Ok, Omegas and Lycan first so we can get their side of the story and get them settled, working lunch with nap *options*, then negotiation, and then we murder the shit out of some bad guys to round out the day?"

"So, they *do* get breakfast," Gamma notes.

"I guess so. Make a note of that when we have to deal with the rights complaints."

"Let's do this," Violet nods, bringing along her own Beta.

Chapter 5 – Establishing Dominance

If you met a crying child in the forest clinging to the body of their dead parent, would the next logical thought be, hm, that child looks like a breakfast-making slave? Would you put it in the dungeon? As a parent, I have a hard time imagining this response. But it happens all the time. Every found Omega has the same story. Somebody important in their life died, and the response from the adult charged with their care - often, the Alpha or Luna - was abuse in *every* ugliness.

Sometimes, Omegas are gaslit with the gospel of 'the gift of service', that their lives are unworthy and only made worthy in the next life by excruciating hard work in this one. Have you met my rude, possibly drug addled, Delta? Even though he is annoying the shit out of me right now, I'm not gonna cast him into a slave pit.

Could fry him first, Ash reminds me helpfully.

Maybe more wolves need to consider therapy, before they turn to enslaving people. Or Wellbutrin, if they *also* want to quit smoking *as well* as abusing their power. Packlands are remote but that's no excuse to lower ourselves. But then again, my Pack is an outlier in every way. The only Pack with a reputation more unorthodox than ours is the one in Hawaii, and the tales of their weirdness border on unbelievable.

These rescued shifters huddled in the guest suite have no reason to trust me, or any of us. Luna tells me that the fact that we have no Omegas has frightened them more - perhaps *our* Omegas are off being tortured in isolation, or we murdered them all. Truthfully, there are former Omegas all around. I just keep zapping the caste aura off of them, on request, although I don't even *have* to. You can be as Omega as you want. Runty little ones. Totally uncoordinated wolfies who trip over their own tails. *Vegetarians.* If I hear about someone discriminating against an Omega, then for *sure* I'm showing up in person with my Luna and both my Betas, to find out why. It does not happen often anymore.

All five of the Omegas we collected are from Blood Moon Pack. It's what I suspected. Their Alpha, Nico, is a bit older, but has weak management disguised by cruelty. Things did not go well for him the last time he showed up here.

The first thing he did was look me up and down, toes to ponytail.

"Alpha Kylie," he bowed, not particularly gracefully. He only sent an emissary to my Alpha Ceremony, so I wasn't too surprised when he arranged a formal visit a few months later. We don't have a ballroom or anything like that, but we do have a decent theater room in the Packhouse, with a little raised stage, so I figured that would be impressive enough.

"Alpha Nico," I answered. I inclined my head only slightly. I was trying so hard to look like an Alpha.

"Luna," he bowed to her as well, "And you two are-?"

"Sisters." I answered shortly, "We are sisters." My first mistake, but we were new to this at the time. "Beta Cole and Beta Brooke," I gesture to them on either side of me. This was my second mistake. "And Beta Olivia," I continued. Luna wanted her own friends, so I granted her a staff as well. Joshi told my father he would oversee us, acting as Violet's Delta, but what he mainly does is play video games with his friends in the Delta Suite all day, and he wasn't even there for this presentation.

Nico observed the three Betas, particularly Olivia and Brooke, with interest.

"You are well advised," he said with a slight tone of mocking, pointing out his single Beta. Wilder, who is a cousin of Easton I was later told, was managing to look both apologetic and commanding at the same time, depending on where you stood at the moment. He *did* execute an elegant bow. I'm sure his master did not see the eyeroll.

"We are well served in many ways," I answered shortly. "And your Luna?"

Nico shrugged as the woman with him stepped forward, but he did not introduce her.

"I have been the Alpha of Blood Moon for 10 years. I was unofficially in the role for a considerable time beforehand, after my father died. You have the gift of youthful energy, but Pack management takes so much more, so much *careful* relationship building. Nuances that can really trip up a young Pack just finding their footing. I am proposing to assist Glacier Moon with some of these more delicate management tasks."

Like I said, I was new. I was searching for the right words to tell him diplomatically to fuck all the way off, but not fast enough, and he continued.

"As you likely know, I searched for years for my fated mate, but the Moon Goddess gave me an incredible gift. She gave me the gift to choose my own." Cole, bless him, he saw it coming while I did not, and he moved subtly from my left side.

Nico sneered to the woman with him, and literally before my eyes, decreed, "I, Alpha Nico of the Blood Moon Pack, reject you, Chiffon, as my chosen mate and as my Luna."

Chiffon collapsed with a yelp of surprise and pain, writhing, but Nico just stood there, with maybe a sharp breath or two to account for the half-severed bond between them. Cole was already down the steps.

Nico misinterpreted his intent.

"She's fine," he said with a dismissive hand, "*She's* not the Queen *my* lands need. What Blood Moon needs is *you*, Alpha Kylie. Join me as my Luna, and we can combine territory and be unstoppable."

He was staring at me with an unconscionable smirk, which is why Cole clocking him in the face with the bottom of a metal stave and then slamming him with a full wolf was such a surprise. My mistake - I should have introduced him as my mate, rather than my Beta, of course. I had assumed *that* was common knowledge! Persia was on Wilder- she's not as big but she is fast, blocking him at every turn and of course Easton and Grant and Olivia jumped into it.

"He is, obviously, what's left of him, going to be escorted off Pack lands," Violet knelt kindly to a heaving Chiffon as I shifted into a firewolf and Ash followed the whirl of fur and teeth out the door, "But you can stay with us here. If you want to be free of him, just reject him back."

I gathered she did *not* want, because when we hurled a *slightly* singed Nico into the trunk of his own Mercedes, Violet and Olivia dropped her on top. He does not send New Years Greetings to me anymore.

He treated his partner with so much disdain, no wonder his lands were a harbor for 'unpaid labor.' Did the Omegas *know* that slavery was illegal? Omegas said that subject was never imagined, even in whispers. And, classic, they had been told when they were trafficked North to my lands, that since they were nothing more than Omegas, they didn't have the proper 'documentation' and if they were sighted they would be turned Rogue and chased into the taiga to die of starvation.

What 'documentation'?

It's not like we issue ID cards.

We can smell you and what you are and where you belong.

So, they had been quietly working and cowering in a freezing basement for *months*. Worse, there had been more of them, but some had apparently been sold away. No surprise, the Lycan had been 'raised' in Nico's Packhouse. Nico was just as criminal as he was lazy. His in-house Omegas met his every need. And I do mean, *every* need. Chiffon got the bonus of her life when he humiliated her - I hope she ran and ran and never looked back.

Chapter 6 – The Lycan

We all have rote speeches, we've done this so many times. I offer them Pack membership and explain that I can, eventually, change their rank. Luna explains that there are many aspects to learning to be a Pack member, and the expectations. My Betas pledge to protect them. My Delta is supposed to offer them training, but where the hell is he? Gamma Grant, randomly, jumps in with his speech about equality and then mentions that a training schedule will be forthcoming. Will it? Where the hell is my Delta? I give Brooke a dark look. She shakes her head.

Eazy, where are you?

Northwards, he says with a grunt, *I didn't think you wanted to be invaded from the North or leave 50 square miles unguarded?*

What I wanted was for my damn Delta to be down here with these damn Omegas, not running off like an arrogant ass.

I am so sorry, Alpha. It will not happen again. Weirdly, I do feel like he's apologetic.

Better not. Hurry back.

Yes, Alpha.

"He's organizing a security patrol in the North," I said aloud to Brooke.

"Why didn't he wait for Joshi?" Violet asks. She made our brother her Delta. He rarely leaves the house, so she was excited to have a concrete task for him.

"Hell if I know," I shrug. He's going to have some hard questions when he gets back here, Brooke or no Brooke. Violet just rolls her eyes. She and her staff take the females out. I motion to the Lycan.

"You stay, please."

"YES, ALPHA," HE COWERS. I mean, he's a sight. He's like 17, full man height, although painfully thin. Dark hair, gray-blue eyes, not unlike my brother Joshi, really. But he's no Naiad. *Wolfyness* just cascades off him. Even Ash, who has fully embraced her Alpha role despite her generally chirpy personality, cocks an eyebrow at this young man. No wonder Nico wanted him out, but to what end? He was totally conspicuous, and only going to be more so.

Of course, the next thing he did was kneel on the rug at my feet and take his shirt off, like I was going to beat him. All I could do was slap a hand to my face.

"Please, don't," I managed. Brooke spoke to him quietly and kindly, helping him up, putting his shirt back over his head and tugging it into place before stepping back to stand beside me. Cole growled lightly behind us. He wasn't upset at Brooke helping; that was Falcon reacting to the slight jealousy *I* felt, watching her touch him. I am exasperated. And aware that this next moment is crucial. Whoever he is, he's going to be a creature of great power, and goddess knows, we don't need his revenge. Hopefully he will save that for Blood Moon.

"What are you called?" Let's start there.

"Levi, Alpha," he is still looking at the floor.

"Levi, where are you from?" Grant puts in.

"Blood Moon, Gamma."

"Before Blood Moon?"

Levi shrugs.

"How old were you when-"

"I don't know how many years I have Alpha. I've never known a birthday."

Oh goddess, he could be any age. REALLY wish I had my Delta. If this kid has already shifted, and he knows less than nothing about controlling his Lycan, there is nobody better at wrestling unruly wolves than Easton. He's like basically a dog even in his human form, and I say that with all the love in my heart.

GREAT!

So great. Who is gonna foster this mess while we get him sorted out? Who do we have who is gonna leave this guy alone; he is so *touchable*. And *I* am saying that, and I am *not* the one who wanders around, looking for someone to touch. Cole keeps me way too occupied for that.

"Grant, take him to Ellie." She is a being of rational detachment. She might stare at him until he is uncomfortable, but not in a lustful way. And if he gets unruly, she won't think twice about throwing him into a pond.

Ash yelps backwards at the idea, and I reach out a hand, with a fire flicker, to catch myself. Brooke is there to steady me.

"Levi," I recover, "We are welcoming you to Glacier Moon. You are invited to be a member of our Pack, but it will be a priority task to help you discover your people and past, if you wish it. I am housing you with my sister-"

"The Luna?" he mouths in disbelief, and horror, and I'm guessing that whoever Nico has as his partner now at Blood Moon, Levi hasn't had the best interactions with her, either.

"No, my oldest sister. She is a *physician*, and a quiet, calm, thoughtful person."

"Yes, Alpha, I will serve your sister well," he whispers. I cannot, with this kid.

"You misunderstand, Levi," I say with a smile, although he recoils. "You serve no one. You are a guest, and we are on probation with *you*. Hopefully you will decide to stay."

"Or?" Barely audible.

"Or not. There's a whole beautiful world to see, in the lower 48 and beyond. But if you are going to travel, I would suggest staying here through at least May. Most of the cross country roads are closed this far north. It's not impossible, but not recommended."

Levi just gapes at me. He has no idea what he is, and what will happen once he accepts that he is free. No amount of snow will prevent assertive visitors.

I wonder how long we have.

"Someone's a fan," Cole says conversationally to his sister as Levi goes out of the room with Grant. "I'm surprised you didn't keep his shirt as a souvenir, the way you acted, falling over underage Omega Lycan! Were you gonna offer to put sunscreen on him next? Braid his fur? Roust would have taken his head off."

Lycans were considerably stronger than normal wolf shifters. "Probably not," I considered.

I don't know what Falcon said to Ash, but I heard her say, indignantly, *No harm in just looking!*

Cole flashed his eyes. He checked his watch, "Define 'working lunch?'"

"I'm skipping lunch and I'm going to bed," Brooke said. "See you at 3."

"Sweet Lycan dreams," Cole catcalled after her.

"Stop," I said tiredly. "I have to go by Luna's office to get the daily reports and then-"

"No," Cole shook his head. "Delegate. Someone brings you the reports, and someone brings the lunch to our rooms."

"And which of these tasks do you volunteer for, Beta?"

Cole gives a lopsided grin, pulling me in by belt loops, "My job is to take you to bed. Because, I want to go to bed. With you."

Ash leaps about, pleased.

"Well," Goddess, this man. "Let's see what we have time for after we have lunch with the kids."

Chapter 7 – Pack Justice

Of the 12 security employees who drew a salary from government funds, seven are implicated as part of the trafficking scheme by the Omegas. Two are identified as the ones who took the others away and they never came back. Those two are going to watch their friends walk into dark, icy water and be dragged under in a splash of terrified gurgling. My mother knows how to make an impression. They will wait to the end for justice.

Grant is a sweetheart. His job as Gamma is mainly to be my law library and external conscience. He's big and he's strong, but he is not and has never been particularly aggressive. He looks very uncomfortable holding one of the metal staves.

Easton should be here; this is his element.

"Where the hell is Easton?" I mutter.

"I talked to him," Grant answers, "There's some complications he is obliged to address."

On the one hand, the complication might be some kind of stupid trouble that only Easton would wallow into and which I would never approve. On the other, the best person on my team to manage him, outside of Brooke, is Grant. I trust Grant's judgment. I narrow my eyes at him, letting out a breath of irritation. *Whatever he's doing, it will keep.*

Right now, we've got bigger fish to drown.

Brooke sets down the final lantern in the circle.

"YOU WILL REMAIN HERE IN THIS CIRCLE." I inform my two special detainees, "AND WATCH THE PROCEEDINGS."

HAHAHAHAHA! YESSSSSS! Ash loves the Alpha voice. *DIE SHITHEADS!*

That leaves five.

"You will approach the water, one by one, and answer the question. If you do not answer honestly, these are the last stars you will see. If your answer does not satisfy, these are the last stars you will see." I'm not using the Alpha voice. They do have a choice.

"Or, you can run." I wish my Delta was here. He DELIGHTS in tackling runners. But, it's been awhile since I've gotten my paws dirty. I am ready.

I hope at least one of them runs, Ash snaps with anticipation.

Part of *me* wanted to run when my mother arose out of the inky midnight pool. She nodded to me and Violet. She is darkly beautiful, wavering in the moonlight reflected off the snow; my sister is her shadow. Violet confers with her in a muted tone for a moment. Hopefully she will come to Pack breakfast in the morning- Autumn and the boys miss her.

Our detainees smell like pure fear. There's a good amount of submissive whining and a lot of pee. Not unlike the Omegas, I note darkly, as I get my wish. Cole staves the first one into the pool; Persia and Ash maul down the first runner. In the end we got two that way. And to my surprise, my mother spares one.

"There is more to the story," she says simply, rinsing Ash off in the moonlight pool at the end.

She is getting downright merciful in her old age.

"Thank you, mother. Will you come back to the house with us?" I contort into my own body, shrugging into a robe.

"Shortly," she nods, erasing all the blood that mars her shrine.

Chapter 8 - Navigating

"Grant," I crooned softly the next morning, standing across the desk from him in my office. "The only reason that I haven't hauled Easton back by Alpha Order and thrown him in a cell is because you vouched for him. So, I suggest that you tell me exactly what is going on. Right. Now."

"Yes, Alpha," Grant responds. But he pauses longer than I can tolerate, choosing his words carefully.

"YOU WILL ANSWER NOW." The room reverberates with my voice. The whole house is gonna know I'm taking someone to task.

Grant bares his neck. I would feel guilty if I wasn't so pissed off.

"Eazy would prefer to stay out of proximity to the Packhouse."

Attorney answer. "WHY?"

"He has to make a painful decision and he wants to think about it at least 30 miles from the Packhouse."

"30 miles from the Packhouse? *What*? I realize Roust is defiant of authority, but anything that requires him to be 30 miles from me, his Alpha, the Alpha he is charged with protecting at all times, is not workable. Not to mention, his *wife*."

Grant has met the basics of the Alpha order, so he doesn't offer me anything further.

"If I drive up to Northward right now, myself, what am I going to find?"

"From what I can tell, an effectively organized volunteer commission and a long line of relieved citizens ready to confess. They had quite a little enterprise taking root up there. You could thank him."

"You could take a look at Brooke, and then tell me to thank him for *that*. What is it about Northward that he needs to be there?"

"Northward is just convenient," Grant shrugs, "He needs a job to do away from the house."

There's a pause.

"What if I send Brooke up to him?"

"I don't think that's great."

Alpha voice again? It takes a lot. I can't believe this asshole, one of my best friends, is putting me through this to protect *Eazy*.

Tired. Let him just sit in the Northwards chasing his tail and then fire him when he gets back. Ash is annoyed.

I feel like I owe Brookey a little more than that.

You know who owes Brooke an explanation? Her mate.

She's been talking to Falcon, who has been talking to Cole. He said the same thing.

"Is he...running around on her?"

"I don't think so."

I stood up. "Grant, I'm not playing 20 questions with you. It's actually really simple. You need to direct me, right now, as to what needs to happen to get Eazy back to the Packhouse.

Whatever he "needs", I am willing to hear it. But he *needs* to be back here by morning, at the very latest, or I will send for him to be *brought* back against his will and that really will make him *significantly* uncomfortable."

We stare at each other for a long moment, until Grant looks away and inclines his head.

"Name two things, right now, that can be done for him?" I want to make *zero* special exceptions for this guy. I am doing this for his *wife*.

"The Omegas need to be placed out."

Chapter 9 – Fated Mates and Chosen Mates

A ll the pieces slot into order.

OH! NO, POOR PERSIA! Ash pulls back.

"Which Omega? Which one is it?"

"Dark hair," Grant mutters, "Arielle."

"That's his fated mate?" My heart sank. Grant does not confirm but he doesn't need to.

Brooke has never admitted if Easton is her fated mate or not. Since Cole and I marked each other before our daughter was born, we didn't expect to have to go through the ordeal of sniffing out a fated mate. Cole, two years older, worried about it when he turned 21. But nothing happened. And nothing happened when I turned 21 either. He, and Brooke both, smelled like they always do. Like vanilla and berries. Doesn't matter what shampoo we use, what cologne I buy him, there's a deep, rich vanilla that I can kiss off his skin. It's lighter, more to the summer strawberry side, wafting off Brooke, but since she is my best friend and the only way I could see her for most of high school was to bring my daughter to their apartment, I guess I spent so much time with them both that I can smell her, too.

I asked Brooke once, what Easton smelled like, after her 21st birthday when she should have been able to scent him out. She did NOT say 'whiskey and mud grass', but I thought maybe that's because Ash just doesn't find him as endearing as she does. Easton would have liked to claim her before then, but her father insisted on chaperones. He was taking no chances on another teen pregnancy. The morning after her birthday they were both marked, so I assumed they figured it out.

But if they marked each other, why can he smell his fated mate now?

"What is he gonna do?"

"He's going to reject Arielle. Of course he's going to reject her. He's not going to leave Brooke. But he's trying to be respectful of the optics, of rejecting a Fated Mate who is an Omega. Of what that *means* to an *Omega*-"

Fated Mates mean everything to an Omega. It's the dream they pray for on every star and with every lit candle. Someone who will embrace them and not abuse them. Maybe someone with a higher rank who will rescue them and make their lives less horrifying. But what they actually get, almost universally, is painful rejection. I don't force fated mates to stay together, that's a nightmare, but Violet and I try to encourage mates to get to know each other at least a little bit before that knee-jerk, OH MY GOD ANYTHING BUT A FILTHY OMEGA, reaction.

But this is different. He's already claimed.

It is different. He is claimed. And I get why he needs distance. And doesn't want to explain to Brooke. And doesn't want to hurt an enslaved Omega, either. My heart hurts for all three of them. The girl doesn't know who it is, just that it's someone who was with the rescue group. And Easton doesn't know who it is; he fled. But there is no way for them to reject each other without meeting in person. And Brookey...

I zip through scenarios. I know the girl he is talking about. Awful pixie haircut enhances the delicate lines of a pretty face. She must be just 21.

I hate her! Ash growls.

That's not fair. Although it's hard not to instantly dislike this girl I've only seen once. *It's not her fault. What does she smell like, to you?*

Heartbreak and ruination.

Stop. I need to know.

Ash pauses to consider. *Different from Brooke. Sharper. Ginger. Turmeric.*

Grant looks just as pained, "Respectfully, Eazy is strong, but that draw is going to drive him to distraction. I don't think ordering him-"

"Oh, he's coming back," I dismissed him. We are not running from *anything.*

"His mate?"

"His *mate* is upstairs, quietly collapsing!"

"So is Arielle." Grant says lightly. I have a tiny flicker of thankfulness that this happened to Easton as opposed to Grant. Easton is black and white, right answer/wrong answer. No matter what, he knows he has to choose and accept his choice. Grant would be *forever* trying to justify both options and we would be stuck in limbo. Luckily for all of us, he *is* partnered with his fated mate.

I rub my eye, calculating.

"Please inform Luna that Arielle is to go to our father and Tevin, and you make *sure* she gets there. I will make sure the Omega classes are not arranged in the house for now."

He leaves the room and so do I.

I KNOCKED QUIETLY. I don't know why, there is no door in this territory that can be barred to me, but we were friends long before our work relationship. She doesn't answer so I push the door open. I can smell her in the bedroom at the back of the Beta suite. She's pretending to be asleep but she is a terrible liar. Always has been.

I sit on the bed next to her. She has a blanket and a big sweatshirt and her long red hair is an unbrushed nest. She's not supposed to be here. She's supposed to be teaching a class, but she begged off.

"How are...you look like misery."

"Thank you, Alpha," she mutters, diving under a pillow. She can't see, but I am grimacing. This is hard.

Let's make mimosas and then just blurt it out drunk! Ash suggests.

I don't think I can toast to this.

"I ordered Eazy to come back."

"Ok," she says, mortified that her mate has to be ordered back to her.

"There's a problem."

"I know."

"What do you know?" I clarify.

"I know he doesn't drink coffee." She punches the pillow away from her face, clutching it to her chest instead.

"Okay?"

"He hates the smell. He's always complained, it smells like farm manure. It's what Rogues smell like, to him."

She fusses with the blanket. I remember the way I leaned on her when I was fretting about being a mom at 16, exhausted with a new baby, my parents divorce, my siblings being water shifters, and the Alpha title looming over me. Through it all, she listened. It's my turn to listen, now.

"So, at breakfast, when he was holding the mug to his face..."

"He didn't drink it. He was just holding it there." She gestured.

"And you knew it was to block the scent?"

"I guessed. He was so slow to get back to the truck, Ky. I really did think he was injured. And he drove back so slowly. I couldn't believe it. He was irritable and we snapped at each other, he wouldn't let me check him and he wouldn't let me drive, but he would not speed up no matter what I said. Roust cut off Persia and wouldn't talk to her at all. He stayed *forever* in the shower. Shifted and made *Roust* roll in shampoo."

Oh my goddess, no, Ash responded with revulsion.

"I thought maybe he had gotten something on him at the bar that was grossing him out, that he couldn't get off, but I couldn't smell anything different."

"What *does* Eazy smell like to you? I thought he *was* your -" Easton turned 21 the year before Cole and Brooke. But he wouldn't have scented Arielle yet - she was 5 years younger, not even in our territory besides. And he certainly kept hanging around Brooke.

"He smells like -" sad tears trickled out. Ash was losing her composure and she was going to take me over and shred the shit out of the pillows in her agitation.

He smells like tannins and dirt and green grass! Aoh screamed at me, *And he smells like he is hurting our best friend!! She is SAD and she is going to be ALONE!*

He would not do that to her. She will not be alone - she has us and Autumn and the boys, anyway.

March that girl into the pond and make her reject him or be dragged to hell! MAKE HIM.

*It doesn't work that way. Her **name** is Arielle and she didn't do this on purpose.*

This is not about her being an Omega! She could be a weirdo Zebra shifter or something else weird, who cares? But she is hurting our friend and she is hurting our stupid warrior and you have to stop her!

Brooke couldn't answer me, she could barely get a breath through her sobs. I did have claws in her pillow, which I guiltily retracted.

"He smells like love and comfort and security," I finished for her, wrapping her in a hug. It didn't *matter*. I *believed* it didn't *matter*. The 'Moon Goddess,' whom my mother disparaged daily, was lazily making matches with a bingo ball spinner rather than any deeper soul based connection. Plenty of people found happiness with a partner well outside their 'fated mate.'

But, the psychic connection, that was real. It might be a little less consuming, *because* he had a chosen mate, but that scent would indeed drive him mad if we didn't do something about it.

What he smelled like to *me*, as we heard the door open and he dropped his leather bag onto the floor with a slam, was sweat and blood, not his, and *shame*. Clearly, he had been distracting himself with work.

Easton nodded to me shortly, catapulting himself onto both our legs as he lay heavily across the foot of the bed.

"I can smell *you*," he said softly to Brooke. "You smell like strawberry milkshake, my favorite thing in the world. It's the only food that Roust likes more than meat, as well. I could never get tired of it. I never will."

What does Ari...the other one smell like? I asked via mindlink.

I can't. Easton answered, *I can't talk about it. I don't want to know her name until the final second, which I know is terrible and against everything we believe. I am barely holding on, Alpha. Thank you for getting her out of the house but how soon can I reject her?*

By this point, he rolled back to free our legs, and bundled Brooke into his lap, whispering to her quietly.

Let me see what I can do. I look forward to hearing about all this blood.

There's a lot to tell. But I have to get my head in order first.

UUGH! Ash screamed at me again. *LET'S DO IT NOW!*

"Welcome back," I said aloud, walking down the hall and pulling the apartment door closed behind me.

Chapter 10 – Control

Easton and Brooke

"I am so sorry Brookey," Easton cracked out. She was looking up at him from the bed. "Please, I chose you. I marked you. You're the one that I love. I don't love this girl. But I can't get her smell out of my head!"

He rubbed his temple, looking exhausted and filthy. Brooke was really far too stunned to trust herself to say anything. She was well aware that this might be a farewell speech.

"I never thought of her, never looked for her. I'm sorry to say it, but I wish we never went there, never found her."

"That's not fair," Brooke countered softly, "Who knows what they had planned for her next. You saved her life."

He groaned in pain. Roust was not tolerating this situation well, and despite Easton's high degree of control, Roust was threatening to overtake him constantly. What the wolf wanted was the security and affection of Persia and Brooke; he wanted to be held and petted and be *a good boy* with them. But he also wanted to own and mark and protect the Omega. And he couldn't understand why Easton was unwilling. It seemed like a stupid human restriction. Would Persia be mad at him? Probably. Would she get over it? Also, probably. He had not intended to be a one-girl wolf. And, really, he wasn't. Easton had dated before he met Brooke. Had been a bit of a player before he fell in with Brooke. But then he got involved in their weird exile, and the ongoing battle over the Alpha title as the Alpha's children came of age. It was chess with living pieces, and one of them had red hair and smelled like berry creamsicle.

We are not going to disrespect the old Delta, Easton had tried explaining yesterday, desperate to get Roust to understand.

Delta knows what makes us strong.

It's definitely not putting your dick into someone else.

As the old man pointed out at the time, you disrespected the shit out of him, messing around with his daughter behind his back. I've overlooked dozens, a hundred, of 'someone elses'. This one isn't just the cute barista who gives you eyes. She is a female who is only completed by us. Why would you deny her that? YOU CANNOT DENY ME THAT.

Because, we marked Brookey and Persia, promised that we would deny a fated mate. I didn't even think they were real!

THAT IS A STUPID HUMAN THING TO PROMISE. Why should I have to suffer your regrets now?

I don't regret it. Please, please stop. I am so exhausted.

I know, Roust answered wickedly, *Have a drink, maybe that will turn me off?*

No, Easton sighed. *Until we reject her, and then hopefully you will stop acting like a middle school teen.*

WE WILL NOT REJECT HER.

Wait, Easton had said, with a pained breath, *Wait until you have to explain this to Brookey. Wait until you have to see her face. Wait until Persia never wants to touch your filthy fur again.*

We are big; there's lots of me to share, Roust answered, but slightly quieter. Persia, and Brooke, were indeed a slight obstacle. Technically, they outranked him. Physically, they were powerful. She was the daughter of the old Delta and she spent all of her late teens waiting for 21 and freedom. She was *not* what Roust could smell on the Omega - desperate, frantic, *frenzied*, wild...

Stop, Easton begged. He was spending all of his energy on outwitting his wolf and his wolf was winning. The last thing he wanted was to dump any of this on Brooke, but he knew there was a limit to bullshit excuses his Alpha would accept before he was dragged back. He was trying to outlast Roust, because Alpha would likely clap him in a cell, and that would at least prevent him from running around town after this Omega.

He wondered sometimes, how he had ended up with Roust as his wolf.

Easton as a teen had been reserved, interested mainly in work, hoping for the Delta or even maybe Beta, in one of the change administrations, but worried that he wasn't well known enough. He was an excellent trainer, but he was not hugely interpersonal. He was a friend of Joshi, but Joshi was also quiet, and mainly liked to play video games rather than train or study. Easton went out for drinks sometimes, but more often not. That all changed immediately on 21 and meeting Roust. Roust wanted to go *out*, and Roust was interested in *company*, particularly *female*. He picked up both experience and a reputation in short order after 21.

And also confidence, because Roust was not easy to manage. Unlike his shifter counterparts, Roust often chose to speak out loud rather than only with the other wolves. It took a while for them to battle out a working relationship and the main feature was that *EASTON* was going to be the one in charge. But there was no shutting him up.

IT WASN'T LONG AFTER 21 when Roust caught sight of Brooke by chance on one of her short treks out of the house.

Never seen that one before. Where has she been, the redhead? Get closer!

Nope, Easton informed him, *That is the Delta's daughter. And he is homicidal and her brother is in trouble, so no go.*

You wimp. You want someone else to snap up the redhead? Go on, go!

We've got a schedule.

Yeah we sure do, we got a schedule to meet a little redhead like the big bad wolfy that we are...

No. Easton watched her go by with escorts.

How do you get that job?

You don't mess around with all the unmated wolves, Easton answered with a hint of amused regret.

Roust considered this and tried a new tactic.

She never gets out of the house, right? She goes to school and she comes home? So maybe she could use a nice friend?

Oh do you know one? Easton said sarcastically.

Happens I do, Roust answered with quiet calculation. Before his age 21 glow up, Easton was an absolute loser, to Roust's perception. He did his work and he didn't even think much about mates. Roust *could* tone it down a bit, maybe meet this girl and unleash The Nice Guy on her until it was time to pounce...

Currently, he was so worked up, he would pounce on just about anything.

"Please hold me," Easton whimpered, holding Brooke's face in his hands and touching his forehead to hers, "Please, I just need to feel close to you."

Maybe, scenting his wife would help. He slipped a hand down her neck and over her shoulder. She leaned in against his chest as he flipped the sweater off over her head. He held her, inhaled her, felt her fingertips tap lightly across his lips. Brooke ignored the stickiness of his skin, and the thin coating of grit that clung to him.

"Brookey," he whispered desperately. He had been plagued for days with unremitting sexual urgency. Roust was angry with him for playing this game, for inserting a girl he didn't want in place of the one he did. But he was a sucker for her smell, for the gentle mocking way she nibbled his chin and his mouth, and her familiar contours. He ran fingers down between her shoulder blades. Every touch felt like fire over his body, he was so hyper aroused. Easton fiddled clumsily with her jeans.

Girl, Persia told her, *You better give the performance of your life, because it may be our last.*

With one hand, she guided his fingers as she flicked the buttons open. With the other, she held his face against hers, returning his kiss forcefully. What did he smell like to her? Right now, earth and blood and panic. He slid hands around her hips, loosening her jeans so he could yank them down her legs. She did everything she could to hide her revulsion.

She had worked to seal this relationship for years. In school, she *liked* Easton, liked the look of him. She noticed him as a studious go-along guy, two grades ahead. Part of the group at school, but not a leader, until his shift at 21, and then she *really* took notice. Gabe isolated her and Cole through their senior year, and graduation, and threatened to keep it up until 21 when he could safely deliver her, *unmarred*, to her 'fated mate'. Easton was the only one she knew brash enough to defy her father's rules. Not at first. It was slow going at first.

They chatted a few times, around the Packhouse. She was truly so starved for contact that she used any pretext to touch him. She wasn't even sure he liked her at all - he prioritized work, often made excuses, denied her the physical connection she so desperately wanted. He didn't even *belong* to the Moon Goddess, and neither did *she*, but because *Gabe* did, he didn't want to even flirt with her? Roust wanted to savage her and move on and she had to fight against his suspicion, too, that maybe she was just desperate for a rough lay to piss off her father.

And *now*, after all the *time*, after she had quietly convinced him to visit her at home with her niece and Kylie and her brother for months, after he had *finally* given in to her back at his bachelor studio, defied her father *twice*, after Persia came at 21 and he stayed up all night running with them and then made her scream with delight, she'd had no *idea*, *and* he marked her, after they marked each *other*, he could be drawn away by only a *smell*?

He won!

She didn't go with the Moon Goddess, *he* became the Delta, *he won*. Was he even thinking of *her* right now?

There had been encounters that were more for release than mutual pleasure, on both sides. But Brooke had never felt *used* by him, ever. She never felt like her body was just a convenient object for him to handle to get off. It wasn't a lack of wanting-clearly he wanted her now, was desperate to have her, but she was subbing in for someone else. Resentment killed any arousal on her part, no matter what he licked. She was reluctant, and he didn't *notice*, unlike him.

Quicker the better, Persia amended her earlier opinion. Brooke agreed.

He was bent over her, but it was a quick pull of her hands to kiss him under the jaw, with a little nip that made him groan, and then turn him onto his back. She rolled astride his waist, bearing forward to bite his lip again, before flipping to face his legs, flick of her hair over her shoulder. Brooke touched her fingers to her tongue, and then ran them down along Easton' dick. He convulsed, hands on her hips. She steadied herself with his knee as he spread her wide with his legs and she slid slowly down the length, and then back up. She was relieved, both that he could not see her face *and* that this would be over shortly. He really only had time to run his hand down through the curls of her red hair once and then grab for her hips again before he arched back, shuddered and done. She faked it admirably, she thought, leaning forward to kiss his knee and extricate herself. He pulled her backward to lay over his chest, crossing an arm over her shoulders. She hugged herself, one hand on his wrist, fighting tears with measured breaths.

"I'm not going to leave you, Brookey," he mouthed, exhausted.

Four, she could not turn off the voice of memory. She had studied Lunar Rites for so long, memorized every word, and it came back in this moment so strong that it overwhelmed

Persia's protests, *To seek solace outside of Fated Mate is to rend the connection with the Goddess, to drift unmoored with no hope of harbor.*

Chapter 11 – Heartbreaks

Back to Alpha

I made it back to my office. Cole looked up from the club chair where he had been sitting with some papers. He knew all my expressions, even my quizzical ones, and he sat me down in the chair across from him and wordlessly made me a drink.

"Just out of curiosity," I swirled the glass before taking a sip, "What was on the original schedule for today?"

"Usual," he shrugged. "The Southern Schools District wants to discuss literacy programming, Climate Committee has a new slew of concerns about glacial retreat along the Western edge. Northward wanted to discuss illegal drugs but we have a bit more insight into that situation now. Budget fights. Gibbous Moon wants to discuss buying solar arrays from us, and there are like 40 miles of frozen sewer causing some concerns. Landfill *is* frozen, like every year...trash trash, money money, complaining complaining."

"Easton is back."

"Ok." Cole nods, not sure of the implications. He's heard a good deal of my wrath related to my Delta the last few days. He's aware of his twin's distress. But he doesn't know the truth. Or my fears.

I throw my head back to search the ceiling for better answers, "What did you think of the Omega with the short hair?"

"I didn't," Cole shrugs, "I was trying to keep an eye on the Lycan."

So was I. He's very distracting.

"Her name is Arielle. 21. Former Omega slave in Blood Moon. And, she is Eazy's fated mate."

"What?" He almost loses control of Falcon in that moment, contorting half into wolf and then back again. "No way."

"*They* are *chosen* mates," I confirm, meeting his eyes. Cole is stunned.

He blinks at me. "Oh my goddess, *Brookey*..."

"He says he's going to reject the Omega; I'm sorry, *Arielle*. She has a name. He told Grant that; he told me, too. But he is struggling. The pull is insidious."

"Let's do it then; where is she!?"

"Cole, I can't just drag her out into the courtyard and put her through that. We've worked so hard-"

"He's not rejecting her just because she's an Omega! He's married, to my sister!"

I shook my head, "I know, trust me, Ash wants to push her into the pond with my mother. But I need to speak to her first. I need a plan of some kind. And it's gotta be fast, because Eazy is gonna find her."

"And then what?" Cole flares up, thankfully he is not a fire shifter.

"I don't know. I don't know, Cole. I don't know how powerful that pull is or what happens if you try to resist it. I don't know that a desperate, defensive Omega can't manipulate him. What if she does look like a lost and forlorn little big eyed Bambi to him and he can't bring himself to do it? You know how soft he is with Autumn!"

Cole repeated, slowly and deliberately, "You don't *know* how powerful that pull is? What do you mean, you don't know?"

"Are *we* fated mates or chosen mates? We did all the things, but we didn't wait until 21, and of course I woke up next to you on my birthday, and we...," after meeting Ash, shifting for the first time, running around all night, we napped a few hours and then...we had been very late to breakfast, "But..your scent didn't change. To me."

"So?" Cole raised an eyebrow.

"So, what if you or I are next? What if the next Omegas we fish out of the back of a truck...or what about all the strangers that will be swarming all over as soon as that Lycan is turned?"

"Kylie," Cole says with complete seriousness, "We are fated mates. I know we are."

He touched the mark at the crux of his neck. I felt lightning on my counterpart, which truthfully did calm me.

He shrugged, with a smirk. "Did you think I dated freshmen in general? Or friends of my sister?"

"I mean-"

"Yes, your father was the Alpha. But there was every reason to think that Ellie was about to be Alpha, and Joshi her Delta. You and Violet were most likely to be paired with an outside Pack. Dating you, no offense, was to risk the wrath of the Alpha, the Alpha in waiting, my own father, *and* the Alpha of a neighboring Pack."

"You did get the wrath of your father."

Cole didn't pause, "Plus, it's not like you were some kind of, I don't know, Fabergé egg that I carried off in my claws. I ran into you, first day of junior year, smoking weed behind the school with, let's remember, *Grant*."

"Grant wasn't smoking, he was asking questions for the purposes of scientific enquiry."

"Same difference. Ripped up tights, ripped up jean shorts, Joshi's old combat boots."

IT WAS LOVE AT FIRST SIGHT! Screams Ash, ever the romantic.

"Aww," I reply sassily to my mate, "It was love at first sight."

"It was *something*," Cole answers with a wag of his eyebrows.

"Are you trying to say I was an undateable horror and by some miracle of being my fated mate you dated me anyway?!"

"No. Trust me, I have very fond memories of the band room at school *and* the skirt you were wearing *that* day. I realized that even though I had seen you around the house for years, I had never really looked at you that much before. And once I did, I couldn't look away. Were we a little young? Yeah, ok. Was I sure? Completely. I knew it was you."

We were so young, actually, that we could barely mark each other. We barely had fangs because neither of us had wolves yet. But the marks hadn't faded.

"In retrospect, we might have been just a touch more careful." Birthing a baby at 16 was a pretty rare thing. It changed the course of the Pack - I was no longer eligible for dynastic alliances. This pleased my mother immensely, who was very against any kind of paternalistic power structure. She also liked to flip the middle finger to the Moon Goddess and her condescending insistence on 'saving yourself for your fated mate.' Of course, we didn't know then that every one of my siblings was going to be disqualified.

"I don't know that I could have stopped wanting you if I tried," Cole replied, "I can barely keep my hands off you now. So if that's what it feels like, the persistent draw like a magnet, then I have every sympathy for Eazy right now. I've been unsuccessful fighting against it since I was 16."

"Ass," I rolled my eyes.

When I considered it, I had always been drawn to him. As my dear mother pointed out, just because I had his baby did not mean I had to stay with him. Even his mark on me wasn't enough - she had a mark from my father the Alpha and look where that led. But as I said at 16, there was nobody else I could even bother with. There was Grant, but he was a bestie. Friends of my brother and Violet, great, fine whatever, but I wasn't interested in taking huge risks to be with any of them. Not like I was willing to do for Cole. And he *had* proved himself.

Chapter 12 – Love Blossoms

First Day of School Flashback

"Kylie, Grant," Cole said with playful, shining eyes, as he trotted around the corner of the gym building in the weak afternoon sun. "Rough first day?"

He was with a few of his friends, other juniors she knew from the Pack. She hurriedly hid her hand behind her back, but Grant fidgeted nervously.

"We don't *care*," Cole said with continued amusement. Something about the blonde, one of the Alpha's twins...she hung out with his sister at the Packhouse. He had been out all summer on the Pack run. Alpha was hoping to pass the title to his oldest, Ellie, so he ordered an inventory of the entire territory. *He* was the Deltas' son, so he was not *nobody*, but he was junior of the members invited. He mainly looked after the camp with the other juveniles looking to prove themselves before their first shift. Maybe he felt more confident, suntanned, taller, after weeks in the wild; he tried a small amount of swagger, nodded his head to Kylie and Grant, and sauntered off to soccer practice.

"Whoa," Kylie giggled at Grant.

"What? Him?"

"I think Coe got taller."

Grant giggled as well.

"Hot summer crush!"

"He went on the Pack run with Joshi."

"I should have gone," Grant said forlornly, "But dad said I was not old enough."

"I heard Olivia say it was rough at times," Kylie answered consolingly.

"So was visiting my grandma." Grant said through gritted teeth.

Kylie dissolved into giggles once again.

"C'mon, you're gonna get us caught. Let's go."

Was it her heightened awareness? Or was there something about Cole? Until this summer, she saw him almost every day at dinner, and often in the common room or in the Delta apartments watching tv with his sister. He was part of the run of Packhouse Children, the dozen or so that lived in the building for various reasons.

Kylie did seek Cole out in the dining room at dinner that evening, and made sure to look up when he took his leave from the room, so she could measure him against the doorframe. Definitely taller. He almost had to duck. That was it. Growth spurt. She wouldn't even notice in a day or two...

"You ok?" Violet ran her hand across her vision, trying to track her gaze.

"Great!"

"GREAT! PASS THE BREAD, THEN!"

"How did your schedule turn out?" Brooke asked her in the hall outside the dining room after dinner.

"Meh. How was soccer practice?"

"Great! First game is tomorrow." Some years, they just painted the goal lines over the snow but it was impossible to play in the never-ending squalls.

"Oh I will definitely come to that." Kylie said, feeling odd as she said it.

"I hope you do," There was Cole, sparking a smile down at her, "I came to get you, Brookey. Dad wants a chat."

"That sounds bad," Kylie commented. Delta Gabe was an unsmiling man.

"First day of school," Cole shrugged.

Brooke nodded earnestly, not seeing Cole's laughing snap of his teeth as they went down the hall.

"BOOO, am I going to vacuum the dining room by myself? We have duties!" Kylie called after them, in vain.

But *somehow*, the next day at the back doors when Cole nodded his head to say good morning, he *somehow* slid a hand around Kylie's waist.

"I like your shirt," he said, from just a little too close.

"Thanks. I'm not sure yours fits."

He pulled his hand back, pulling down the edges of his purposefully slightly-too-small polo.

"See you at school." He left her to wait for Brooke.

Is it possible, that he could smell her? That shouldn't theoretically be possible. She smelled like patchouli, *and* weed, and like the vegan glycerin base of her hippie Luna mothers handmade soaps. But that's what the Alpha apartment smelled like most of the time, unlike the Alpha offices, which smelled like Aqua Velva.

But *she* smelled like pumpkin pie spice, he couldn't name it, kind of underneath it all? He tried to think about math, because there was a test first period. Not that he did any of the summer studying. He counted a billion Caribou, did that count? How much calculus did he really need for that?

Cole found himself looking for her in the stands at his soccer game. She was there, with Grant and her sister and some of the other freshmen.

Brooke kicked him a ball and he missed it, in his distraction. He scrambled back down the field to regain control.

"It's funny to see Alpha's twins in the high school," one of his friends commented in the locker room afterwards, "It makes everything seem much more real."

Cole gave him a quizzical look.

"Alpha retiring next year, your dad retiring. It will be weird, all the officers being college age. It sucks for us, honestly. We will miss the cut off. Joshi probably won't change, if he even notices. But those two little girls will have nothing to do but pour tea for dignitaries sent to scout them out for some other Pack."

While he was sure Kylie could entertain in a pinch, Cole doubted Alpha's youngest daughter had diplomatic hostess aspirations.

He hadn't really considered before, that Kylie and Violet would probably leave the Pack. That was of course true. Alphas second sons from varying Packs had been turning up a lot at Glacier Moon in the past year, trying to make an impression on Ellie. Very likely, her Fated Mate was one of them. One of them was probably Kylie or Violet's Fated Mate as well, considering. Moon Goddess consistently matched Alpha offspring. The only thing she liked more was toying with Omegas and linking them to Alphas, apparently as a kind of personality trait determination test? They got rejected, some very unkindly, one hundred percent of the time.

He was a Delta's son; he could be Fated to anyone. Into an Alpha family? Probably a bit of a jump. If it was anyone in his acquaintance, it was probably Gamma's daughter, Olivia. Or else an Omega. His dad would be pleased, with a competitive athlete like Olivia. But his dad would also be pleased with an Omega, if it came to that. His mother had been an Omega, and as far as Delta Gabe was concerned, there was no greater act of fealty to the Moon Goddess than to share worship with a worshipful Omega. Everyone knew, Omegas were her heartblood.

He resolved not to be so nosy about Kylie. She was just another freshman girl, friend of his sister, and her time in the Pack was ticking towards an end. He prayed to the Moon Goddess to Fate her somewhere warm, with seasons.

He tried to remember this, vividly, when her mouth was pressed against his. They were half hidden in a pillar gap between ranks of lockers. She was fine boned, and her fingers across the back of his neck felt both icy and hot. He was losing it over this girl. It had been like 2 weeks into the school year. He managed to shift his focus back to soccer and school for like maybe one whole day, but then Brooke invited her back after practice, and while his sister went to change, he somehow managed to walk by Kylie getting a bag of microwave popcorn from the pantry.

"HEY!" He growled, to be funny. She jumped, she dropped the bag; was she surprised or did nothing surprise the Alphas daughter? But he apologized, picked up the packet and put the popcorn in the microwave for her. Before it beeped the first minute, he had impulsively kissed her, cupping her face in one hand.

She stared at him, mouth open in surprise. Cole appraised her, with questioning eyebrows. Then he nodded his head shortly, reaching sideways without looking to pop the microwave door open.

"Popcorn's done." It wasn't. But he handed her the half inflated bag in the silence, shut the microwave door, and then left the apartment and went to Joshi's room to watch him play video games until he felt much more zen and less shaky. All the weed in the world couldn't cover that spice smell that he couldn't place. Luna must be dipping seasonal candles or something; it was everywhere.

Kylie was fully still like a statue until she heard the door close behind her and then she dropped the popcorn for the second time, and ran with a little yelp to Brooke's room.

"Are you ok?"

How to answer that question? Brooke had to ask again, with real concern.

"I'm fine, I'm gr—ok. Just, Cole...just...kind of...I don't know...kissed me?"

"What?" Brooke blinked.

"In the kitchen."

"Like, on the mouth? Romantically?"

"Sort of? Yes?"

There was a pause.

"Do you object?"

"I...*guess*...not?"

"Is he still standing out there? Like a fish? Having a stroke?"

"No, he left, but Brookey...what *now*?"

"I don't know Sweetie, I guess you have to ask him. Or slap him, depending on his answer. Where did he *go*?"

"I don't know!"

"You were standing there in the kitchen and he just walked up to you, kissed your face, turned and left?!"

"I mean, there was popcorn, but yeah, basically!"

Brooke could see the half-popped kernels scattered near the abandoned bag.

"You want me to hunt him down?"

Kylie considered. "Is this like a thing he does, or like, the Summer Run unlocked some kind of *urges* or what?"

"I mean, maybe. He's 16 so all of them are completely made of *urges*. But, he has been kind of interested in you all week. He's been waiting to say hi to you on his way out, dressing a bit less sloppy, giving me the update of where he noticed you at school. He *tends* to notice things so I didn't think much of it, but now I realize he wasn't just burbling on randomly like he does - it's all been about you." She giggled, "He's herding you like a Caribou!"

"Oh, my goddess."

"Well, do you like him back?"

"I don't know!"

They both giggled, but then Brooke's face fell.

"It kind of doesn't matter," she said quietly, "I'm sure he does like you, Kylie. But he is not your Fated Mate. I know we won't know for sure until at least 21, and maybe longer, but, with your dad," she shrugged, "Your mate is not going to be in Glacier Moon, anyway, right?"

"My mom doesn't put a lot of faith into Fated Mates," Kylie answered after a moment's consideration, "And, I'm 14. It's not like we have to get married, after one kiss."

"No, no, I know but..." Brooke went to a lot of Moon Goddess Reflection classes.

Cole had been skipping quite a few Moon Goddess Reflections. And he was glad, because half the Pack was at the Shrine on Sunday, when he finally ran into Kylie again.

Had he been looking for her in the Packhouse on purpose? Yes. Did he have a plan for what happened when he found her? No.

He was idly walking by the Packhouse library, on his totally casual and not at all suspect tour through the property, when he glanced into the room and saw her. She froze, brown paper shopping bag hanging on her wrist. She was restocking the handmade soaps to the bathrooms around the Packhouse.

He kept walking a few feet down the hall, got hold of himself and backed up. On second glance, she was gone. He went into the library.

"Kylie?"

No immediate answer, but there were no other doors. Should he pretend that he didn't know she was hiding in this room somewhere?

"Kylie?" He tried again, more quietly.

"Yes," from the dark bathroom.

Cole walked up and hit the light switch. Kylie was affecting to arrange soaps decoratively on the counter. He spared her the knowledge that she had darted into the dark bathroom to hide.

"So, um, about the other day, in the kitchen-"

Kylie looked at him blankly.

"Do you, maybe, want to, come out of the bathroom?" He paused.

"I'm just delivering my moms soaps."

"Yeah, actually can I have one? Whatever spices she is using right now are amazing." Cole stepped backwards, so Kylie could exit, and she handed him a brown ridged bar wrapped in a square of printed fabric.

"She always does these for fall."

"So, the kitchen-" he started. The bar smelled intoxicatingly amazing and frankly neutralized some of his anxiety. "I hope you didn't think I was-"

"Serious? No, I didn't." Kylie said nonchalantly, swinging her bag.

"No," Cole considered, " I was going to say rude. I *was* serious."

"Oh," Kylie breathed, "I was surprised."

"Sorry, I was too, a little. Surprised that you kissed me back, at least."

"I did not!"

"You did!" Cole's eyes crinkled at her indignation, "I had to leave to-."

"What was that about, anyway?"

"Dunno," Cole shrugged, "I kind of think I like you."

Kylie blushed an intense red.

"Is that...ok?" He hoped so because her scent was all over the house in the form of these soaps and he would not be able to hold another thought in his brain at the same time.

"Yeah, it's ok. Just, you know, I'm not staying at Glacier Moon. I'm leaving the Pack one day, so-"

"No, you're not," Cole said, impulsive once again, grabbing her by the wrist just above the twisted paper handle of the bag and pulling her in for another kiss. This one she did reciprocate.

And it had been intensely hot and heavy since. Not gratuitously gross to the point that people were avoiding them, but every secret minute was snatched up and they were clearly an item. Cole knew it would not be long before he heard about it from his father and was made to serve some penance to the Moon Goddess.

Chapter 13 – Traditional Views

Back to Alpha

"**B**ut didn't you think," I asked, "That Eazy had that for Brookey? Why would he hang out in the boring old Delta apartment with us if he didn't have to?"

Every time one of my siblings came of age, Brooke and I got our hopes up that with a new Alpha she and Cole would be released from the Delta suite of rooms. Unlike my mother, Delta Gabe was *very* sure about Moon Goddesses, Lunar Rites, and saving oneself for one's Fated Mate, and he was *very* upset by my 'single-handed seduction' of his son. He couldn't do much about it, so he took it out on Brooke. She went out the door for school, and every day there would be escorts to make sure she and Cole went directly home afterwards. Cole had a tight childcare schedule - he split parenting with me, but per Gabe he was not allowed upstairs in the Alpha Suite with me and Autumn. Sometimes he toyed with his escorts by taking our daughter to the park first. What were they gonna do, keep the Alpha's grandchild away from the swings in case I was waiting there to get pregnant again? I could *visit* them at his place, and I left Autumn with him overnight several days a week, but they were not often allowed out.

We made an *effort* to look totally overwhelmed and exhausted whenever Gabe was home, when we were caring for our daughter, but truthfully there was a lot of 'naptime'...and Cole's right, I couldn't ever stop *wanting* him. All he had to do was slide a hand over my arm and I automatically nestled up against him. The rule about not approaching me in public without express leave was in part due to this tendency.

"I think he did have that for Brooke." Cole confirmed what I had always believed. Why else would this older dude voluntarily join the Delta Apartment Exile? Why chase this shut-in girl? He was already training for the security job, he was a busy guy and well liked in his cohort. He was a good friend of my brother, and would have been on his staff.

I throw my hands up. We wouldn't be in this perilous holding pattern right now if Cole's words were really true, right?

Cole laughed, "*Love*, little miss 'Moon Goddess is a Chauvinist'. Just love. He *just* loves her. She *just* loves him. Like normals. You believe in that, or don't you? Are you secretly in league with the Moon Goddess now? It's fated mates or nothing? You gotta whelp some pups or nothing? That would be quite a reversal on your part. *Yes*, I do know that *we* are fated mates, if it matters. You are absolutely stuck with me and anyone coming up here to carry you off is going home in an urn. But I *chose* you as well, and that's enough."

"And the half naked waif, groveling at your feet, begging you to save her, covered in scars, pleading, *please Beta, only you*, while every atom of your being is shrieking to touch her? How do you defend against that?"

Ash growls at the idea. I take it Falcon is keeping quiet.

"Love, has that ever worked on me?"

"No, but it also doesn't work on Eazy!"

"No, it doesn't work on *Easton*. It works on *Roust*. I don't think you paid him much attention before 21?"

"I knew him from Joshi, but no, we didn't hang out."

"He was not like this. His personality is much quieter, analytical, more like my dad."

"Delta qualities, yes."

"And then he turns 21 and suddenly he's chasing every skirt in the Pack."

"Ew."

"Roust gives him a huge boost of strength and bravado, but he would have lost everything if he wasn't so disciplined. Eazy is in control, making use of his wolf's gifts. Just like you, *Firewolf*. He already beat Roust once. He's not gonna lose this time."

"He's tired. He can't stay awake forever. Also, covered in blood for some reason?"

"See? He's great at dispensing justice."

"What is *justice* for his fated mate *Omega*?"

"Being freed to find the person who loves her for her personality and not just because she smells like maple sugar and allspice."

"She smells like ginger and turmeric."

"That's what *you* smell like," he reminds me, "Maple sugar and allspice. Hint of coconut. I can taste you from here."

Goddess, I melt for him every time. Somewhere, there's a parallel universe where I am not the Alpha and our lives are not this complicated. But what about Brooke and Easton?

"What if, in the face of an onslaught like that, love is not enough? My parents-"

"Your parents' situation is incredibly complicated. And Eazy *loves* an onslaught," Cole reminds me.

"He was so feral, Coe. I'm worried."

"You have a thousand roles, Ky, but minding the love lives of other adults is not one of them. If he ends up with the Omega, yes, it will hurt Brooke. It will change our staff dynamics. But the sun will rise in 6-8 weeks, and she will be ok. She will be free to meet someone else. Maybe have a family. Things change and that is ok. That is the freedom in being Chosen rather than Fated."

Nico's smug face jumps into my thoughts; for him, the freedom to choose was the freedom to exploit. Has Easton fallen into that trap, too? I am so saddened by the idea. Everything is so comfortable between all of us; why does that have to change? There's so much drama in the work of the Alpha- can't I have a drama free personal life? And what happens if I have to choose between Brooke and Easton as officers? Cole stands up, wrapping his arms around me and inhaling my hair.

"Can I kiss you, Alpha?" He asks softly, an inch from my lips, seeking my mouth. He doesn't have to ask, here in the privacy of our own space. His calm does settle my anxiety a notch. Ash is purring in a most unwolflike way. Cole smooths my hairline and lays down a last kiss before stepping away.

"Where are you going?"

"I know where they hide peppermint oil, and I am going to concoct something just *brutal* for him to smell. It's gonna blow his olfactories right outta his head."

"I do need him to be basically functional. There's a Lycan to manage," I remind him.

"Maybe a touch of Allspice," he winks, "Not right now. Right now, he's useless until you read the Miranda Rights to the Omega and persuade her to give up her claim on him so you can have the moral high road."

"*Moral high road*?"

"If the roles were reversed," Cole said, "And some male was slavering over Brookey, I don't think any of us would blink an eye when Eazy shredded him. To that end, if it was the Lycan you ladies are wetting your panties over, I don't know that you'd be so protective of your reputation. The Bambi eyes work on you, too."

"She didn't do anything wrong."

"Sometimes that doesn't matter."

Spoken like a true Delta's son.

Cole winked, "I look forward to *maple sugar* later this evening, my Alpha."

"All you can eat, Beta. Enjoy your science project." I give him a dismissive wave, adjusting my clothing as I head to the desk.

Chapter 14 – Brooke and her Goddess

Flashback

On Sunday afternoons, Brooke went to Moon Goddess Reflection. She just turned 20, this was her last year. The topic for the final Reflection season was Fated Mates, and all the ways to show devotion and appreciation to the Goddess by worshiping their forthcoming Fated Mate. Cole flat refused, and also refused to take his daughter to the toddler programs, so Brooke went, as usual, as the family offering. It was grating, but an excuse to get out and she often met Easton, *accidentally*, while trooping over the snow.

One week, he went to the gym early to be back in time to meet her, jogging back up the freezing building stairwell, but stopped outside his door. There was a noise.

Its Little Red, Roust answered his silent surprise.

She's supposed to be at Reflections? Easton drew his eyebrows together, hand on the knob.

Yeah, but also, I can smell her.

She's not 21 yet; don't be ridiculous.

Suit yourself, but there's a nekkid redhead, smells like Twizzlers, in your shower, and that's her.

I guess they finished up early, Easton hesitated in the hall.

Dude, what are you waiting for?

What am I doing with this girl? She's in my shower? Doesn't that seem a bit...?

Like an invitation? You object to her taking her clothes off?

Maybe.

Easton went in. Brooke had been interested in him since they were in high school together, where he was two grade levels ahead. It was a small school and they were both on the soccer team as well, but he was a senior while she was an underclassman who sat on the bench with her brother. If he thought of her at all, it was with pity. Everyone in the Pack knew that her brother had gotten Alpha's underage daughter pregnant; neither of the Delta's teenage twins were around much after that.

She maybe had a bit of a crush, engineered reasons to be around him. He 'ran into' Brooke in the Packhouse, or on the school grounds shared with the training facility, much more often than he ran into other girls. He had enjoyed the attention a little, the distraction from fretting over the competition to be an Officer in Joshi's staff. He visited her and her brother and the baby sometimes... maybe regularly... in the stifling Delta apartments, but he *was* already around to see Joshi and his other friends.

After Joshi's birthday came around, *he* was too busy trying to cheer up a crushed demigod, and feeling sorry for himself. After wallowing in his own disappointment, he was ready for release when he finally turned 21.

ROUST ROLLED IN, AND he forgot all about the schoolgirl in the Packhouse for a while. His shower had been a *parade* for the first few months after his birthday.

Easton knocked on the door of the tiny bathroom, wondering when he last cleaned it properly.

Last weekend. Roust supplied. *Instead of getting laid.*

Do I have a clean towel?

You do laundry every Thursday. Instead of getting laid.

"Ma'am," Easton drawled in his security voice, edging a towel around the door, "You may have dropped this towel?"

No answer.

I wanna see, Roust whined. Easton cleared his throat, and knocked again.

No answer.

"Brookey?" He opened the door a bit. The room itself was small, with just space for a capsule shower, toilet, sink. She was there, rinsing her hair, and she looked over her shoulder at him over the top of the slightly rusty metal divider.

"I thought you had Reflection?" Easton said, folding the towel over the barrier between them as she turned the water off and gave her hair a twist. He kept his eyes on her face *only*.

"There was a test."

"How did you do?"

"Aced it." She wrapped the towel around her hair. Easton wondered if that was on purpose, or if females normally needed two towels? But she opened the door to the shower stall and stepped out, naked, into his arms. He kept a little distance between their bodies, not least of all because she was covered in cold droplets, but did lay his chin against her smooth forehead for a long moment.

Take this girl to bed already. Clearly she wants it.

I'm gonna need you to take a break; this is a people problem

This is the kinda people problem I am more than willing to solve and where I frankly excel.

Not here, not with her. Bye.

You wait until she gets her wolf.

That is exactly what I am waiting for, thank you, bye now.

"Did you know," she murmured into his shoulder, "That there are 22 scribed ways to please a Fated Mate as a reflection of the Moon Goddess?"

"Is this what you've been studying?" Easton asked.

"I know them all," Brooke informed him. She seemed quiet, kind of withdrawn. She didn't move to kiss him, which is what he expected. He was scrambling for the right answers, not sure what Brooke was intending. Maybe she just wanted a shower?

Welcome to decision time, Roust told him with exasperation. *Do you have a good reason to push her away right now?*

"One, greeting your mate upon every meeting with the deference one would offer the Goddess herself." She blinked up at him.

"Like, should I bow?" Easton tousled the towel off her hair, wrapping it instead around her body. He dismissed the vanilla and strawberry scent as an implanted memory from Roust.

Come on, man.

He pulled her forward the few steps out of the bathroom.

"Two is conducting oneself with humility, as Fated Mates have positions of great authority over us, as the Goddess does, and we do well to recall our unworthiness before them." Brooke answered, in a prim, slightly sad voice.

"Oh no," Easton shook his head, "This stuff is awful."

I don't hate it.

"Three," Brooke kissed her own fingertips, and then touched them to his lips, "We do not speak our desires. Fated Mate, like the Goddess, knows what is best for us and will allot to our needs accordingly."

You cannot. Let them. Do this to her. This is how they keep the Omegas in line.

In the little studio apartment, they were right next to the pile of her neatly folded clothes. He could reach the stack on the bed with one hand. He could either dress her, or he could...*not.*

It may be too late. Easton hesitated. *Giving her over to the Moon Goddess is the only thing Gabe has ever spoken of with a smile on his face.*

You've already got a future date for another beat down from Blitz just for continuing to speak to her after he told you not to; you might as well make it really worthwhile.

"I don't even want to know what four is," Easton pleaded, "Please Brooke, I know this is important to your family, but you have the right to your own...happiness. Body. Whatever you want in the future."

"Wrong," Brooke corrected, in the same stilted voice, "Future only lasts as long as Fated Mate wills it. They speak for the Goddess. When Fated Mate is lost, we serve others instead, so they may know the happiness that is lost to us forever, until we return to the stars to serve her again."

Explains her father's cheery outlook. Her head is stuffed full of all this controlling Moon Goddess nonsense, she's falling in love with you, and she knows you don't feel the same. Time for goodbye! Just rip off the bandaid and show her the door.

No!

"Not all of them are terrible," Brooke said, after a pause, in her normal voice. "Thirteen through seventeen are all related to the things permissible to say *to* a Fated Mate *while* being mated in the acceptable position, with some particularly intricate incantations to say while being marked, specifically."

She can't blame us, Easton could hear the shrug, *You haven't given her any reason to think you're into her...*

Other than sneaking out to meet her every week, inviting her here?

Oh yeah, and sucking her face off every chance you get. Just thank her for coming and send her home. Then we can catch up at the bar! They haven't seen me in weeks! And there's bound to be some new faces; we owe it to them to see if any are your fated mate, right?

Easton cleared his throat. "What if I'm not your fated mate, Brookey?"

"Then you will leave me when your person comes to be with you, and I will drift unmoored with no hope of harbor."

Rubbish. She doesn't buy this trash either. Why would she? She's been raised with Luna. There's a goddamn Goddess.

Easton was 22, and the previous year had been a wild one. He had never been a devotee of the Moon Goddess, never went to Reflections, and he was ambivalent regarding Fated Mates.

Having one thrust upon him would save him a lot of effort. He would have been fine with an Omega. But Delta's daughter was enamored of him, she should not be, and admittedly, he was attracted to her. Just being her friend was a difficulty, given lockdown. He tried to keep his distance, but their polite peck on the cheek of greeting had progressed to full hungry kisses that he felt with a zing all down his body.

That's just carpet static, Roust dismissed.

He kissed her now, hesitantly. Brooke melted against him.

*I don't know why you think you're doing her a favor, denying her the thing that she knows that she wants because **you** think you know better than she does. Delta should be pleased at what a good little Moon Goddess adherent you turned out to be.*

Shut. Up.

"I'm not gonna leave you, Brookey," Easton kissed her face, lifted her up, and set her on her knees on the bed. One hand traced from her neck, over her shoulder, and down her body to her hip. Her fingertips on his waist, sliding up his shirt over his chest, slid away any resolve he had left. If she was aiming to seduce him, he was going to make it worthwhile. He had hesitations, but he wasn't made of self-denial, either.

Roust stayed out of it, but was secretly pleased that his stupid little man-cub finally made a conquest of his own accord. He was soft with her, but that was because he was stupid. Rather than doing the sensible thing in the situation - providing the pounding she was begging for and then letting her quickly move to greener pastures as a confident woman, so that he was *not* the one her father stabbed when he found out- this fool just fell into actual infatuation with the girl, ignored her bids to take the relationship physical, and then went and took her anyway. With no wolfy coaching, why even? What was he supposed to do to amuse himself if this was the only one he intended to vanilla-style bang until her father inevitably murdered him?

She did smell nice.

Why did you let me do this? Easton demanded, with a naked Brooke cuddled against his chest under his sheets. He kissed her damp hair, ran a hand over her ear and down her arm.

You told me to stay out of it. Roust drawled.

I'm not her Fated Mate!

She doesn't seem to mind. The door is right there - you can reach it from the bed. Open it, throw her clothes down the hall, let her go. There's been a good number of warm bodies in that place. You didn't freak out with them. At least not after the first few...you're out of practice and you just need more repetition, is what I think. So pat her on the head and tell her you'll call her later. Then don't.

This was complicated enough.

She's not to your taste? Fine. You're not into amateurs; me neither. Try out a few other flavors, maybe circle back to this one again later, because she honestly smells delicious. The world is your oyster.

Easton growled a little. Brooke opened her eyes with concern, and Easton pulled her in tighter.

No. What I'm committing myself to is keeping her safe until her fated mate comes for her.

The daughter of the Delta 'kept safe' in your bed? If that's your delusional narrative, no shifting and making it my problem when Blitz and this 'fated mate' both beat your ass.

"Hey, you're shivering!" He smiled, and to his relief Brooke smiled back. She didn't have a wolf yet, so the cold affected her more. "I'm happy to keep you warm, but eventually someone is going to notice that you slipped your lead."

"I am so tired of the Packhouse."

"You can always come keep me company, when you get too bored. And we will find other ways to get you out, other things to do. I'll see what I can arrange with the training schedules."

"A whole year."

"And then what?"

Brooke shrugged, "I don't care as long as I can move out and walk around town without being reported."

"It's not that long. Just a little bit more."

Until what? You give her away at her wedding?

"We might need to jump back in that shower real quick so you smell more like shrine and less like the apartment block to the Delta," Easton said with an eyebrow.

KYLIE SWIVELED TO LOOK out the window, and then back to Brooke as she came into the Delta apartments.

"Is it raining?" She asked doubtfully. It was dark outside, it was usually dark, but she didn't hear rain. It was generally too cold to rain, anyway.

"Melted snow," Brooke answered, hanging up her coat. There was a slip-second of hesitation that gave Kylie pause. She glanced at the clock.

"Easton walked you home from Reflections?"

Brooke leaned down to scoop her niece, and headed to the fridge to check for snacks. They found cheese.

"Mhh Hmm."

With strong side eye, Kylie leaned on the counter, "How was Reflections?"

"Short."

"Really? It's 6 and you left at 2:30...what's there to do at the shrine, all this time?"

"I was with Easton."

"I hope nobody saw him walk you home."

"I finished the exam in 15 minutes," Brooke whispered, "I was *with Easton*."

"You were *with*," she glanced at her daughter, who did not appear to be paying attention, but who did like to repeat things like a Mynah Bird, "*The security trainer* for more than two hours?! OH! *OH*, no wonder your hair is wet!"

Brooke poured herself a water, took a sip, gave over her cup to her niece.

"So.....how was it?"

Brooke nodded, small smile.

"You went to his apartment?" Kylie paused, thinking of Easton in the physical sense. It was literally impossible not to see every adult member of the Pack full frontal naked outdoors at some point. He was roughly the same height as Cole, maybe more filled out since he was already shifted and often running around with the security team.

"That's ok," Kylie pursed her lips impishly, "It fits a bed and that's all you need! Half the Pack probably saw you...*heard you*," she teased. Kylie was serious for a moment, "Are you ok, though?"

Brooke blinked, and leaned her head sideways, "Yes."

Kylie held up a hand, "No, I mean, I know there are Lunar Rites *rules*...it's sounds like you kicked them all over on your way to jump into his sheets."

"Into his shower..."

"Wow, you left the shrine of the virginity goddess, and then what, asked to use his bathroom and then just took your clothes off instead? I didn't realize you moved past the making out stage!" Kylie had been in that stage for maybe a *week*, four *years* ago. She and Cole now occupied a state of constant entanglement. Although, that still wasn't easy, between childcare, work, school, and actual chaperones if the Delta was in a particularly controlling mood.

Brooke visually indicated her niece, placidly eating her cheese.

"I'm sorry," Kylie retorted, "*The mommy daddy kissy kissy face* stage -"

The door bowled open and Gabe came in. Kylie stood up.

"Hi Grands," Autumn continued humming her cheese song.

Gabe nodded to the group, "Spoiling our dinner with snacks, I see. Kylie. *Brooke*, I spoke to the priestess on the way in."

Brooke went white and rigid. Both Kylie and Gabe noticed.

"She said you had high marks on your exam today." Gabe tried to smooth over what he assumed was testing anxiety with a smile. Brooke's mouth turned up into a smile, but her body did not relax.

"It must have been a hard one," he offered. She must have studied and worried; no wonder she was so anxious over it, his good studious girl.

Brooke nodded.

"Well, good work."

Neither girl answered. Brooke only nodded, retreating to the far corner of the little galley kitchen.

Chapter 15 – Easton Detained

Back to Easton and Brooke

Easton and Brooke were not doing much of anything, sitting together on the sofa in their suite. Easton was uncharacteristically clingy, partly out of exhaustion and partly out of fear. If he walked away from her, like to get a drink from the fridge, he would *keep* walking, down the stairs to the street and he would find the Omega...

OUR MATE, Roust asserted.

And reject her.

Roust snorted. He couldn't say what he wanted, because Brooke was draped against Easton's shoulder and Persia would hear and she made it clear that she would never be First Wife. She had also offered him a *taste* of what he would absolutely never get again, man or wolf, if he gave in to his base desires. Satiety, after days of being on edge, did dull the constant bolts crashing across his body just a crumb.

COLE KNOCKED AND CAME in, flicking on the lights.

"Rousty," He held out a ball, "Looka what I got! Whadda got? I gotta ball!" He tossed the ball to Easton, who caught it in his hand, sniffed, and retched *immediately*.

"What is that!" Brooke scooted back across the sofa, hand over her nose.

"Thanks to a hot tip from Falcon," Cole answered, "*That* is a pomander of Peppermint, Cinnamon, and Clove oil."

"It smells awful!" Easton held it away from his body, doing everything he could not to slam open the window and pitch it off the deck behind him.

"It does. I aerosolized it with a spritzer. And the tiny pinch of Wolfsbane doesn't help, either."

"Ugh!" Both Brooke and Easton recoiled.

"But," Cole continued, "Did it get Rousty to settle down a touch?"

Easton blinked, gagged again, and looked around, probing his mind. Roust, after days of being so feral he was basically wolf in a skin suit, had retreated. And the sharp ginger and muddy turmeric that had been a waking nightmare all around him was blessedly gone. He managed to smile.

"Oh my goddess," Easton stared at Cole, "Thank you! I *hate* it, but thank you."

Cole gestured at a double layered ziploc back by the door.

"I made a few of varying strengths. I can't even stand to be near *me*, right now, and that is after a shower, but we just gotta hold on a little longer, ok."

"Ok," Easton nodded, taking another sniff and regretting it. It made his head spin.

"You guys ok?" Cole asked. Brooke and Easton looked at each other. Easton's relief was evident.

"I think so?" Easton ventured. Brooke answered him with a smile, but neither man noticed it was only with her mouth.

"Interfering *moon* goddess," sighed Cole. "Naiads are superior all the way, in my book. You missed an epic carriage of justice on some of the Northwards guards who turned out to be actually assholes. Luna Kyoko issued some *judgments* from the shrine pond. Two did a runner; you would have loved it."

"Sorry I missed it. Turns out, they were trying to make meth up there. And there's a weird exotic animal black market and quite a bit more sex work," he paused, looked at his wife, and cleared his throat, "Than expected."

"It gets dull in winter here."

"I could use for it to be more dull, right now." Brooke commented quietly.

"I'm sorry," Easton said again. He'd already said it a dozen times. "I feel *very* dull."

"You probably need some sleep." Cole crossed his arms.

Easton shook his head. "The minute I do, that lunatic is gonna be running the town."

"Well," Cole said, "We call them cells, but they are actually pretty nice..."

"It's what I was kinda hoping for."

Thank goodness, Persia said darkly.

Persia-

No sweetie, I love that stupid dirty dog, you know I do. It's been a while since I've seen him like this. He's addled right now, and he'll return to rights soon enough, but don't you want him to just shut up a little?

Brooke didn't answer her.

I know you don't feel good about any of this, but you did the right thing for him. They needed to feel us, feel secure in us. Smell us. It wasn't his best performance, but I'm sure he's just exhausted. Roust has taken advantage of momentary weakness on Eazy's part, but he'll make it back on top.

Brooke took a sharp breath.

Trust me, Persia said smugly, *That old mop talks a good game, but he knows the prize we are. You married a lion tamer, my girl. He's got control of Roust. He's not walking away from the goddamn Beta, no way.*

"Let me know when you're ready." Cole coughed.

"Coe you don't mean now!" Brooke widened her eyes.

"I do mean now. Like NOW now. I'm hoping you guys kissed and made up, or whatever, but Brookey, you and I are needed. We got 99 problems and Roust ain't gonna be number 100."

"I get it, it's fine. It's a good plan. Just please, can you speed it up with the-"

"Next on my list," Cole promised, backing up and holding open the door for Easton. Brooke stood from the sofa.

"*You* can't do this." Cole informed her severely. "*You* meet me by the truck in 10."

Easton kissed his wife lightly, and she handed him the sofa throw. He smiled in his familiar, laughing way. But Brooke felt nothing but dark foreboding.

"Nice authoritative tone you got there," Easton said conversationally to Cole as he went out, taking the bag of pomanders with him as well.

"You think so? Thanks, I've been working on it. You know who it doesn't work on?

"Your wife?"

"Autumn. Hey, bonus depending on your point of view, you are probably cut off from the mindlink until the wolfsbane is out of your system."

Chapter 16 – Twisted Schemes

Back to Alpha

Luna and I were totally exasperated. This Omega girl was either a diabolical genius or there was a lot of lead piping in her former home.

Pond, is all Ash would trill from time to time.

NO! I sought more patience.

Not coming from me, Ash chided, *Some dogs are not trainable.*

"You want me to give up my mate, so your sister can have him?" Arielle replied tearfully, for at least the 3rd time.

"No," ever-patient Luna Violet is starting to lose it.

"She's *already* married to him. *She* is the Beta. You met her, the red haired female." I have already explained this.

"Your sister?"

"Sweetie, *Luna* is my sister, *Beta* is his wife."

"The Beta. He wants to be with the Beta, and not with a gross Omega." She got very stuck on the fact that my Betas are twins, and one a female. Now that she's figured it out, she will not let it go.

"You are not gross, ok, you are lovely, and.." I was going to say smart but I have limits, "And fun and a *survivor*. And you will survive this."

"*Survive*? Will it hurt?"

Oh my goddess, choose better words! Violet says to me with irritation.

She hit her head on every branch on her way out of the nest, Ash adds.

"It will hurt, a little bit. But it will hurt him too!" I try to reassure. Ash snickers in my head.

"Then he will *hurt* me?" More tears.

"Not on purpose."

"But he will reject me on purpose and that will hurt me and he wants to do this?"

Oh my goddess, is she an attorney?

Oh I don't think so, Luna retorts.

"But forever if I stay here the Beta will hate me? *Both* of them will hate me?"

"No." But maybe, if you don't get your furry tail in gear, girl. We've been through this!

"It's just a mistake. They are chosen mates; the moon goddess confused the situation."

"The Moon Goddess confused the situation?"

"It happens all the time." I continue, missing the withering look from Violet.

"It happens all the *time*?! The *Goddess* makes mistakes? I feel this heartline drawing me in over every obstacle and it is a *mistake*?"

"Haven't you considered that the concept of Fated Mates is a little sexist and patriarch-"

Luna cut me off. "Moon Goddess is very busy and sometimes she looks away for a split second to see how something else is getting along and oops, her hand slips and throws the wrong two shifters together. That's why there is the option of rejection."

I don't think this explanation would work on even my daughter, and *she's* 8. But Arielle seems to be buying it.

"But then will I get a new mate?"

"Usually. Usually you get a second chance mate."

"But will I get a second chance mate?"

Is it her wolf that's this simple?

Nope, Ash answers.

"Probably."

"But not for sure?"

"No, not for sure, but *probably*. And you could always fall in love and have a chosen mate."

"Who is going to fall in love with a rejected pile of garbage Omega that the Delta and both Betas all *hate*?"

"Anyone. Lots of people."

NOBODY wants to be with you, you half witted baby bird. Drown her in the POND!

"This is worse than Blood Moon! I smelled my mate and I was so happyyyy! I thought that was *sacred*! That you two, so different from every other Luna and Alpha, would understand!" She wails, "But he does not want meeeeee!"

"He's not available." It's Cole, entering the room behind me, and his tone is not coaxing and soft, like Violet and I have been using. Violet and I are relieved - that last jab really stung.

Chapter 17 – Arielle's Desperate Bid

Arielle is not giving it up. "I spent my whole life waiting for my mate and he never, never came. *He* never stopped the beatings, or the freezing, or the starving, or Nico's hands. I knew I could survive all that, as long as I could meet my wolf and my fated mate. I just had to make it to 21. I was terrified they were taking me away to kill me, just before I was set to turn. *Dragged* me to this lifeless, icy, waste! And then finally I get pulled out of the basement and he's supposed to love me and he doesn't love me and I get *nothingggggggg*."

"Oh well," Cole shrugs. We all ignore the comment about the natural beauty of Glacier Moon. If you are used to grass and way fewer conifers, it can be an adjustment.

That's so much to put on one person, I comment to Violet.

Yet, they all want to keep worshiping the woman who insists that Omegas are somehow necessary.

Nico would still keep house slaves even if there were not convenient Omegas.

Violet sighs, *Ain't that the truth. Combing the forests for Rogue children, next.*

"I'm all alone! This is so hard. I wish you had left me in the basement! At least Nico wanted me, sometimes…"

"You are just at the beginning of your story. This is not the end. You have a wolf now, and we can help you. But you have to let go of something that is not yours." This is exactly how he talks to our daughter when she is stamping her foot. Bambi eyes really do not work on him at all. "We can just kill you if you want." Cole says flatly, which he does *not ever* say to our daughter. Arielle sobs hysterically.

"Beta, you are not helping." I grit my teeth.

"Delta is detained on your orders, Alpha." He responds, "I suggest we end this chat-"

And *that's* when the door was blown in. Cole and I both shifted, and he got a solid kick to the shoulder that sent him into the wall. Violet fell backwards but dissipated into a small fountain.

Oh, he escaped! Ash growled, swathed in flame, ready to launch. The big male snapped at her and lunged, but Arielle fell over in a faint. He snatched her with a long sinewy front leg and then loped off back through the splintered door. I heard the *oof* of Violet's Beta getting kicked as he sped past.

"You ok?" I called to Olivia as I went back into my human form to help Cole and Violet. Violet coalesced back quickly. Cole rotated his shoulder.

"Just popped," he answered with a wince.

"The hell was that?" Olivia hurried in from the hall to Violet, touching a bloody claw scratch over her arm. Brooke was behind her. She had been outside the outer door and got smacked into a snowbank.

"I think we better check on Ellie."

"Of *course* she fainted," Brooke said with an eyeroll, dabbing at Olivia's wounds, which were healing quickly.

"Be nice," Violet said automatically, although she seemed just as irritated.

Do not address my Beta, thank you. Ellie?

What? Yes, Alpha?"

Are you ok?

I'm delivering a baby right now...

Have you seen your houseguest?

Levi? I left him some books to read and a recipe to follow. Is he ok?

NOPE. I cut the connection. At least she's ok. Lycan probably trashed her house, but she's in one piece.

They are all looking at me now, as I ball my hands into frustrated fists. Brooke and I exchange glances.

"Lycan hunt?" Olivia confirms.

I am so sorry, Beta. I tried. I feel for her; this just won't end.

I know, Alpha. The heart wants what it wants.

No, the stupid Moon Goddess gets drunk and sprinkles fairy dust down without bothering to check first on the mundane lives that she is upending!

"Does *he* want her himself or are they friends and he's just protecting her? And how did he know where she was?" Violet straightens her long skirts.

"Well," Brooke answers quietly, "If he's trying to help her by giving her her heart's wish, he's probably wrecking the Packhouse basement."

Cole smirked, "Easton isn't in the cells at the Packhouse. She's not going to find him."

"Where did you put him?" I ask, news to me.

"Are you ordering me to tell you?"

"No, but I kinda wanna know?"

"Your wish is my command, Alpha, but let's talk to some of our remaining guests from Northwards first."

He has a reason not to tell me.

Chapter 18 – The Traumas of Blood Moon

"Ok," I am so hopeful that we chose well. Getting all three of the Omega girls into one place seemed like an unnecessary waste of valuable minutes, and created a Lycan target besides. So we split up and there is *chaos* in the mindlink.

This child is not even 10, Grant reports from across town, *I don't think she knows anything more than what she already told us.*

Well stop terrifying her and be fatherly! I yell back. *Was she in the Packhouse at Blood Moon?*

There is so much weeping. Violet comments dryly, where she is with Joshi and the Omega being fostered at the edge of the forest. They can travel more quickly over the frozen snow than Ash can even run, so they took that case.

No sign of Levi or Arielle anywhere.

The woman in front of us, in front of Brooke and I, is a picture of misery. She hated her life, but she knew what to expect. We dragged her out of the basement in Northwards, and suddenly she's got a roommate who already keeps an obsessively tidy house and keeps harping on her about asserting her rights and *feminism* and she has very little education and *no context* for what is expected of her now, especially *right* now. She was in a chair but now she is kneeling before us on the floor, head touching the ground. Her foster friend hovers in the background, unhappy with this regression. So am I.

Brooke and I kneel down as well.

"Lyssa," I manage, as gently as possible, trying to do what Violet does, trying to pretend I am talking to my daughter instead of a woman who looks old enough to be my mother.

"It would be a great service to me, as the Alpha, if you could share what you know about-"

"About Her Majesty?"

"Her Majesty?" Is that like, the name of their cat? Surely not the-

"The deposed Luna, Alpha. She styled herself as Her Majesty and wished to be addressed as such."

"Oh-kay. Please tell me about Her Majesty." Violet would die if she knew Chiffon was parading around as Her Majesty, probably still half rejected.

What the hell, I send to my Betas.

What? What's wrong? Cole demands.

Nothing, just this story is bonkers. Brooke replies for me.

"Well...I am sure all this has come as quite a shock to her, Alpha. Everyone knew Alpha Nico was going to mark her, she said so often enough, and he called for her often enough..."

Both Ash and Persia growl softly.

Brooke blinks, "Are you talking about Chiffon or-"

"Arielle?" I finish.

"Her Majesty." Comes the answer from the carpet.

"Please sit up so I can hear you. We are not going to call her that, here."

"Arielle, Alpha. Luna Chiffon has not been in the Packhouse for several seasons."

Silence as Brooke and I both try to work out the connections.

"But she was causing problems for the Beta, and then when Alpha didn't mark her, she just was so upset- she was expecting it, you know. She had been counting on it. She had a bit of a rage-"

I had one second of sympathy for Arielle. It was brave for an Omega to show *rage*. It must have been terrible to think you are about to be free after enduring years of abuse and then have it snatched away, and here we were doing the same thing...

"And then he turned her Omega and sent her in the next shipment to Glacier Moon. I have an old injury in my shoulder, I don't work as fast as I used to, and there are plenty of younger Omegas, so he rid himself of me as well."

"He turned *who* Omega?" Brooke breathed.

"Her...Arielle. She wasn't born Omega, no, she is the old Beta's youngest. She was fated to the new Beta, Wilder, but she rejected him, so she could court the Alpha. He had a liking for her, especially since he was taking something of Wilder. There's never been anything Wilder had as special that the Alpha allowed, going back since they were children, so when she came of age, Alpha claimed her right away."

Good thing Brooke is already on her knees, because she looks like she is about to fall over. I've never known what to make of Wilder - he chooses to serve a vile master. But I do feel kind of bad for him. Maybe I'll put *just* him back on the New Years Card list.

She might be too gross for the shrine pond, Ash considers.

I can't fault her for going after what she wants. And she can do what she wants with who she wants. I am the poster child for that. I can't even fault her for pursuing Nico over Wilder, although they are both disgusting. Nico is a tyrant. There was nothing stopping him from retribution against Wilder, or her, if she didn't comply. And if you're going to bed the nasty creature, might as well get something out of it and aim to be Luna.

"What about the Lycan?" Brooke manages to eke out.

"Who?"

"The boy, Levi."

"Respectfully, Alpha, the sooner you get him out of your lands, the better."

Don't I know it. Even if he weren't tied to this sordid drama, he would be trouble.

"Thank you, that is my intention. But why was he sent here?"

"Wilder. Alpha was going to turn him Rogue and set him outside the territory. The old alpha brought him in as a little boy, but as he's gotten older, he's attracted a lot of attention."

"There's nothing Nico hates worse than that," I nod.

"No, Alpha. Nothing. But Beta Wilder can be a bit soft, within, you know, a cruel kind of soft. He didn't want to see harm come to the girl, no matter what she had done. They were a pair, for a while. So since the Alpha was cleaning house anyway, Beta arranged Levi to be included, and protect Her Majesty."

Ob-nox-ious. I breathe out. I know Easton has done a bit of sleuthing, up in Northwards, and at least one of their trafficking hubs there has been destroyed, but how long has this bullshit operation been in business, and where are the other two girls who were sent on before we found out? Oh, my Nico, just you wait.

WHAT NOW? From Cole, *Little girl knows nothing but keeps calling Arielle 'Her Majesty' for some reason.*

Arielle's definitely an Omega, tho. She scents of Omega. They were getting louder, Cole and Grant, so I knew they were getting closer.

She wasn't until recently. Nico made her one. She's Wilder's mate, but that didn't work out, the Lycan is with her, it's a whole thing.

Wilder? Easton's cousin over at Blood Moon?

She got second chanced to his cousin? That seems weird.

I am feeling considerably less compassionate towards the plight of 'Her Majesty.' I admit. She's been the pilot of her own choices. As strong as that fated mate pull is, as much as it might even represent a clean start for her, she has not been a victim of circumstance like the other Omegas. And there is no "the starving and the freezing," other than what she probably perpetrated herself.

Other than being a member of Blood Moon, where everyone is victimized by their Alpha mutt. Ash notes.

That's not even unusual among most Packs, particularly the ones who are most devoted to Moon Goddess worship.

'Nico's hands' was probably true, I acknowledge.

Don't start that! Brooke shushes me, and then touches her mouth in surprise.

No wonder she was worried about not getting a second chance mate. Have you ever heard of a thrice chance mate?

Well she doesn't deserve mine! Brooke pulls her hands away from her lips, checking her fingers as if for blood.

Are you ok? Let's find her; she's going in the pond. Welcome to your bright new future, Arielle, when I find you, where you are the author of your own story. I'm sure you will hate it.

Alpha voice, ALPHA VOICE! Ash paws around gleefully in my head.

Chapter 19 – Delta Gabe's Lecture

In the Gatehouse Apartments

"Rousty, Rousty, Little Mousie," came the sing-song voice again. Roust was laid out, full wolf, on the floor of former Delta Gabe's living room. Autumn was twirling his fur, using him as a bolster as she watched TV. Gabe moved over to the old guardhouse apartments when Kylie was elevated at 21. He had to admit, his daughter in law had risen to every challenge. She had exceeded all expectations. And his grandchildren were a welcome joy, now that he could spend more time with them.

But he could have killed his son in that first moment when he found out what was happening, 9 years ago. The only thing that prevented him from attacking Cole and giving him a very physical reminder of the consequences of flouting rules was Kylie, clearly heavily pregnant and unfortunately very newly 16, standing beside him and refusing to move. The second he understood what his son was trying to blurt out, he had been overtaken by his wolf, Blitz. And Blitz dug his claws into the granite counter, running his tongue over his teeth for blood. His vision was blurred red.

"You will return to your rooms where you belong," he growled out the order. But Kylie was the Alpha's daughter, and a Naiad's daughter; he couldn't order her to do anything. She simply stood there, unmoved.

He had to content himself with a searing lecture. He said some vicious, hurtful things about the value and intelligence of sex crazed teenagers. He may have used the term 'slutty,' more than once. He could not control Kylie, so he controlled her access to his son, and *his* daughter. He took every privilege from both of his children. They were twins, obviously Brooke had known this was going on; let them share the consequences. Not even Alpha could override his right to parent his own children as he saw fit. Not that he cared to; Alpha had his own problems at the time and was just grateful his Delta was so committed.

Luna Kyoko was a good friend of Gabe, and she tried to intervene multiple times. He was willing to agree that she was a beautiful, powerful deity herself, and he had all respect for her. Of course, Gabe would ensure his son was an equal parent. But, no, Cole and Brooke were not coming out to the Equinox celebrations, nor to the biannual ball. He was an old fashioned man with an enthusiastic respect for the Moon Goddess and Lunar Rites faith of his family, and he was *not* willing to embrace this new-fangled mess-around-with-anybody-you-want and just have a baby, it doesn't matter, it's all fine, lifestyle. Cole had ruined himself *and* a young girl, ruined his chances at an Officer role, ruined his odds to find a fated mate.

And then *this* one walked in to his life. Gabe looked at the big, dark wolf passed out on his rug, being idly petted by his granddaughter. What a stupid color for an arctic wolf, he sneered, ignoring the fact that both of his own children had shifted into red wolves at 21. Easton had been on his radar as

Officer material back then; Delta, maybe Beta, in anticipation of when Alpha's son Joshi took the reins. He was disciplined in training, although he was a bit soft spoken. A wait and watch type. They didn't spend much time together, other than for Easton to receive assignments, but he seemed dependable. Easton turned 21; he was gifted *this* guy.

Roust was not docile in the least. He was large and he was cocky. He was conniving as well. It was a recipe for a swaggering bully. Suddenly, Easton was picking bar fights and there was *clawing* for dominance between some of the unmated juveniles parading past his door. For the Pack's newly shifted, tolerance was extended to 'dating', to search out your fated mate, but *then* there was blatant *disrespect* for the Goddess' intentions, and Easton was certainly at the far end. Roust was a terror. It took a few months, but Easton managed to slide back into the driver's seat, fight back up to the Officer rankings.

But *no* deviant, disrespectful, stinky mess of a wolf was touching *his* daughter before 21. Bless the Goddess, Brooke, *at least*, was promised to *her fated mate*. He would stick her in a Moon Sisters convent if he had to. He knew *why* Easton was suddenly full of pressing work questions, loping up to him while the old Delta escorted his daughter in the afternoons. It incensed the old man; he sent away for Moon Sister convent pamphlets. Brooke could not possibly *be* this young buck's fated mate - she was not 21 for two years, just finishing high school. So he was clearly trying to get up the skirt of the next unclaimed baggage in the line. Shortly later, Blitz made *eminently sure* that both Easton and Roust *understood* that his children were unavailable.

Easton didn't live in the Packhouse, but Joshi did, so it didn't strike Gabe as particularly suspicious that Easton was often in the building. Many of the young would-be officers were trying to advance with Joshi as his birthday got closer. Gabe had been hopeful. He was tired. He was tired of all the insolent adolescents bouncing around during training, and deflecting all the questions about what was going on with Alpha. He could happily retire and spend some more time with this bright, cheery cherub that Cole and Kylie had produced.

And then everything was dashed; Joshi turned 21 and proved to be a Naiad. *Cole* was partnered to the Alpha's last hope of heir. Suddenly, in this new crop of yesterday's children, there was talk of either Cole, or *Brooke*, as Officer material? And Easton was somehow particularly talented at refocusing impudence and distractibility into *enthusiasm* in the younger set? Gabe felt old and defeated as he resigned himself to two more years in purgatory. He was too tired to argue when Easton knocked on the Delta Suite door to see his daughter. If this kid wanted to spend his free time in a well lit, easily observed common area with his twins, a disgraced teen mom, and a toddler, let him.

Blitz had *not* been too tired, however, to thrash Easton when he discovered that mongrel had already been visiting the Delta Suite at off hours for over a year, and worse, had been abetting Brooke to sneak out to *his* lodgings.

All that did was drive her in deeper, Blitz noted with derision. *Just as all our speech did to Kylie and Cole was ensure she would never give him up.*

Well that turned out to be a blessing at least.

His twins were 21 shortly afterwards, and there was not much he could do about it then. They *all* had another year to wait until Kylie and Violet revealed which, if any of them, would take over the Alpha role.

Brooke told him they were fated mates.

They marked each other.

She lied.

She *lied* for him, this big lump of gray fur who wouldn't even *be* here right now if his son hadn't drugged him, he'd be out chasing another skirt, having apparently run through all of Glacier Moon's offerings and moved to *Blood Moon's* eligible females as well.

"'This is exactly what happens when you disrespect the Moon Goddess," he muttered, to the back of his granddaughter. Everything was so simple if you just followed the orderly ways.

"What is?" Autumn asked, only half listening.

"You get big, uncle lumps-on-the-floor who have to be put to sleep like a young pup and babysat instead of out doing the job of the Delta." Gabe answered, jiggling him a bit with his boot.

"Like the babies," Autumn nodded sagely, not looking away from her show.

"Didn't you get enough of a taste of restriction, that you decided you had to have some more? Oh that's right, you were only pretending to my face to follow my policy, so you could run off with -"

Gabe didn't like the sound of pawsteps in the hall. They sounded heavy, and he had the heaviest wolf in the Pack on his floor at the moment.

"Autumn, go to the room with your brothers right now." She sat forward, looking wide eyed at the front door. He shifted, letting Blitz take over.

Roust opened his eyes, stretching, a bit wobbly. Blitz gave him a side nod of dismissal.

No. With a low growl, the bigger wolf gestured Blitz after Autumn. The old white wolf scooped her onto his back and skidded into the hall bedroom, where the twins were napping, closing the door with a gentle kick. Roust remained in the living room, hunkered down and facing the outside door. It was going to take more than a pinch of poison to take down *this* Delta, no matter what the old man thought.

Chapter 20 – The Lesson

Flashback

"Some might call them shrewd, and some might call them crafty," Gabe said conversationally, "And in a dark moment, *deceitful* comes to mind."

"Sir?" Easton hadn't been listening. He was sorting some notes, standing in front of his locker in the training gym. He blinked and turned towards the Delta, but Blitz slammed into him before he fully rotated his head. He hit the locker hard enough to gash his side and bounce into the metal bench with the other shoulder on his way down. Although Roust surfaced immediately, Blitz had already kicked him across the floor and then bounded after, fangs at his throat.

"Delta-" Roust questioned, staying very still. Blitz removed his mouth, sat back a bit, but Roust could tell he wasn't done.

Luna Kyoko covered for her, claimed she had some kind of cold, that's why she's been so jumpy lately. Blitz growled. *But I know my daughter. And I know that she's been quick to run out the door of her Moon Reflection classes so she can find you, dog, sniffing around her in the parking lot. You'll keep your distance, now!"*

Roust fervently prayed to the resident water goddess that this was *all* Delta knew, because being smacked around was one thing, being made into a pelt was another. He was swiftly punched in the face, Blitz's snapping jaws inches from his own, daring him to fight back.

IS THIS WORTH IT? Roust demanded of Easton. *I told you, this is **your** beatdown!*

Don't say a single thing or we are dead, Easton could taste blood.

Get up. Blitz snarled. The rational part of him that realized Easton was not *protesting* the accusations fueled greater rage.

Pack does not need a traitor, nor do I.

Roust got to all four feet hesitantly, kept his head down. In truth, he was larger, heavier, and stronger than the white wolf. He was not so stupid as to believe Alpha would *like* it if he bested the Delta, nor would that help Easton with his girlfriend in any way.

Blitz leaped, bearing him down, locking jaws on his shoulder to thrash him around. Despite himself, Roust yelped and growled, throwing the older wolf off of him.

You've been told, you shabby, foul beast, not to approach my daughter. Nor my son, or my granddaughter, for that matter.

Blitz's claws punctured Roust's chest, pulling him up from the ground so he could yell in his face.

You'll not be warned a third time. You are no longer invited into my home. I don't want to see your sorry ass in the Packhouse, either. I better not see this baggage anywhere near me, or my children, outside of work.

Blitz threw him down.

*I won't scent you around her again, or your line will **end** with you.*

"Understood?" Even naked, hair streaked with gray, heaving from exertion, the old man looming over him projected dominance.

"Of course, sir," Roust choked out. He didn't move from the floor, blood seeping from his chest wounds. Gabe swiveled on his heel, but turned back and belted him across the jaw with a heavy fist for good measure, before kicking Roust's back legs aside.

"Damn," Roust worked his jaw, rolling over from his back onto his paws.

This just got more complicated. Easton sighed.

This just got a lot more fun. Roust snorted, giving a bloody cough as Delta took his leave from the room.

Your nose is broken, Roust confirmed, *Can you try to line it up properly so it doesn't ruin my profile?*

Easton groaned, gingerly grating the bones back into place, trying to stifle the faucet of blood.

Just hold it like that for a minute. Also try to hold your shoulder closed and don't breathe too hard because when you move your chest you keep bleeding from there.

IN THE ALPHA OFFICE, Alpha Mason was busy, standing over his desk and sorting through the papers that Kyoko or Tevin had helpfully piled up for him. He was also listening to Gabe, who had kicked in his door, ranting about his daughter.

He had known Gabe forever, for their whole lives, and his Delta was always ranting. As teens and young adults, he was forever musing about the girl who would be his Fated Mate. He was obsessed with the idea of her, everything she did was good and perfect, the little Omega. After she died, Mason endured a decade of inconsolable grief and anxious parenting worries about raising motherless twins. Then came *rage* when Kylie started dating Cole. Now, Delta was determined to drag Brooke to the finish line at age 21 like some kind of trophy, validation for all the emotional expenses.

To Alpha, who was far more concerned about who was going to inherit the fragile borders, economy, and ecosystem in which they *both* resided, not to mention had fought and killed for, found it hard to muster up interest in a grown woman who was *suspected of* having a friendly conversation with a man her own age.

He tried, for Gabe's sake.

"Sounds like you handled it," He said to his friend across the desk, with an eyebrow waggle.

"Aye, Blitz gave him the standard shake down. He'll not be running after her again."

Mason gestured, "We *do* need him to do his job. Some of the juveniles need remedial training. He'll have his hands full."

"He can figure it out," Gabe dismissed, "Keeps him busy anyhow."

"What does Brooke say? Does she think they are Fated Mates?"

"Please, how can they be? He came from Blood Moon originally, and she 's set to be a priestess."

"Oh that's right, his family came from Blood Moon, I forgot about that." Mason hoped this was the end of the conversation. Gabe seemed calmer than when he slammed in, half shifted and slavering.

Gabe took a breath, "There's no doubt the lad is good at his job, but his wolf is dodgy and I don't trust him one wit. He's the type to take a barrier as a challenge. I want to put chaperones in the apartment again, for at least a short time."

Alpha said nothing, not looking up from his desk for a long moment.

"No," he finally answered.

"But-"

"No," Mason met his eyes. That was really all he needed to say. Delta would never dare to defy him. He offered an explanation only in deference to their long shared history.

"One, we don't have the budget. Two, I am not comfortable diverting resources to a 20 year old adult who is not in actual danger from anything. Protecting the infant was one thing - neither of us knew how the Pack *or* Kylie or Cole were going to handle teen parenthood. But this is over the top, Gabe, and you know it. She's not a little girl. Legally, she doesn't have to listen to anything you say, and I wouldn't have a leg to stand on to compel her to do so. Third, everyone in the security pool is handpicked by Easton. I'm not saying he would defy your orders; I hope he wouldn't, if he knows what's good for him, but why tempt fate? So *no*."

Gabe inclined his head and walked out of the office.

"And let her out of her room!" Alpha called after him, sighing as he turned over more papers. He was thankful that he had never felt obligated to control his children, especially not Kylie, to any 'greater good.' He had enough troubles.

EASTON HAD ALWAYS GIVEN the Moon Goddess shrine a wide berth. It was central in town, a curving building with stained glass windows, constructed of light colored bricks. When he moved from Blood Moon at age 4, his family was delighted to find that there was a competing goddess at Glacier Moon, *and* she was the Luna! The vicious, combative hierarchy that defined Blood Moon seemed to be a favorite of the Moon Goddess, as she was always granting their Alpha's bloodthirsty wishes and greeting his sacrifices with favor. Luna Kyoko, on the other hand, limited her intervention to a totally partisan duck pond game and Reiki booth at the summer fair.

Technically, the basement storage, built under the building and into the side of the hill, was not *in* the shrine. He wasn't sure she was there. There was no light under the door. The only footprints marring the snow were his own. He couldn't smell a thing but choking, smoky incense.

Mlwah, Roust tried to clear his nose as they approached. Easton looked around. In a few weeks, when the sun rose and illuminated everything constantly, this low area in the landscape would not be as private. But in the dark, endless arctic winds scouring his footprints off the snow and blowing his scent away from the Central Locale, a person would have to walk over from the edge of the parking lot and search down through a scrubby line of pines into the ravine to see him. He knocked on the door.

"Hello," answered the redhead, with a smile.

"Hey." Behind her, in the softly lit room, Easton could see stacks of books, supplies, benches. She pulled him in and shut the door. They wanted to send her to the shrine to pray for her soul? Fine; she had all the keys.

Chapter 21 – Roust's Primal Instincts

Easton and Roust

Roust pawed his snout a bit. Damn that Falcon. He wasn't really *permitted* to attack the Beta, but Falcon was gonna get a pawful of peppermint in his goddamn eye just as soon as...

Roust could feel Easton fighting for control of their shape and he batted him down.

You need me for this, for whatever is coming through the door that Delta Gabe doesn't like. Relax!

Then Roust smelled what Easton had already scented - ginger and the spice of turmeric, less powerful than before but still beguiling.

Relax, Roust ordered again. *You are wasting our energy. You know I'm not going to leave this door for anything. But I'd like to see what you plan to do with your puny people arms.*

Our scent is stronger when it's you!

We are well beyond that. I don't think Beta considered the Lycan into his plans.

The handle of the door jiggled. Roust carefully laid back down on the floor, rolling one of the hateful pomanders nearby and trying not to breathe it in. Roust willed himself not to breathe at all, surreptitiously burying his face in the blanket he brought with him from the Beta rooms - deep strawberry vanilla, a touch of bitter tears. He could make it another moment, but not if he got maced with wolfsbane again

"Oh! They drugged him!" Arielle cooed tearfully, rushing to Roust as Levi kicked open the door. He was shifted; she was not. Levi looked over to the TV curiously. He sniffed the pomander on the floor beside Roust. It made him dizzy. He felt blurry for a moment, kicking it away. That instinct was badly calculated - it hit the wall, sending up a spray of clinging oils. Arielle and Levi both yelped back.

Backing down the hall from the smell, Levi recoiled further. There was a low, dangerous growl from behind a closed door. He was not used to shifting, and overwhelmed and fearful, and now he had a stabbing headache from whatever the hell was in that ball.

"Leave it," Arielle said crisply, "Carry him!"

You have a plan, now? Other than pretending to be a rug? Easton demanded angrily, trying to shake off the physical sparks that he felt when Arielle threw her arms around Roust's neck. She was a pretty girl, although the short asymmetrical hair cut wasn't doing her any particular favors. But there was something in her scent, now that she was so close, that he was struggling to place.

We are getting them far from the babies and the Delta, that's the first priority.

He's pretty strong, Roust. You are a big boy and he's not even struggling.

You should feed me more.

Either he's gonna kill us, or Alpha is, so I don't think we have to worry about food much longer.

Don't be stupid, he's clearly helping our Mate, and she doesn't want to hurt us.

What does she want with us?

Oh my, little Eazy, I feel like I had this conversation with you when you were 21. It's very natural, at certain times of a man's life, to have certain urges. Like 5 hours ago, when you were with your wife.

Yes, Roust, with my wife, and Persia. You know we can't do this. There is no Happily Ever After for us here.

Can you just relax and enjoy the moment? Can't you smell this girl? It's the most intoxicating thing, like being drunk. I love it. I NEED it.

That's the wolfsbane.

Maybe. And this guy runs smooth like butter. Imagine if he was not half starved and kept in a cage? When did you ever get snuggled by a Lycan? This might be Happily Ever After right here. Is it demeaning to keep a Lycan Omega as a personal rickshaw?

I feel like Violet and Grant would both say yes. Easton replied, trying to quell his distress. He could force a shift, but it would take a huge burst of energy, and he might need that strength. He knew he was strong, knew Roust was strong, but he was no match for this Lycan. He hoped at least if he went down fighting, Brooke would be comforted that he at least tried.

You're ridiculous. Roust commented dismissively.

You're gonna ruin my life for the second time. Wife, job, home, Pack.

It's our life, dipshit. Don't be such a pussy. We both know I'm the best thing that ever happened in your life.

Maybe besides that redhead. Think about her, Roust.

I think about her all the time. She's a very forgiving person. I take no responsibility for that lackluster performance earlier, by the way.

Chapter 22 – The Moonsnake Trap

Y*ou don't have to mark her, just to...get close to her.* Roust continued.

I will force you out of my body.

And you'll freeze to death, Roust answered, *Seems like a stupid way for a wolf shifter to die. Why crucify yourself over this, a mate who was designated by an actual goddess **for** us? Don't you want pups, like Autumn? Maybe you should go see the shrink. Why are you so afraid of change?*

Because I worked like a junkyard dog to get to this place? Because I am the goddamn Delta? I beat out 60 others for that job.

Or, did she pick you to please her mate's twin? A little present for her favorite.

No.

She could have made you Beta, if you were that good.

I was going to be Joshi's officer, before you even showed up.

Before I made you? I'm just saying, Roust drawled, *there's plenty of jobs where you **don't** take the orders from your wife, and mate's day begins **and** ends taking orders from **us**, instead.*

Easton was quiet.

And what kind of father would you be, Delta? Never home? Wiping blood covered footprints on the mat? Maybe that's why

Beta doesn't want to have pups with you. But this one certainly does.

You're done. Easton decided to take his body back, but the Lycan stopped running.

We're at the Shrine Pond. Roust observed with interest. He was set down gently in the snow; he still pretended to be weak.

Arielle knelt next to him, stroking his great furry head. Internally, Roust was fighting not to be overtaken by her scent.

"You won't reject me, right? I know I'm only a lowly Omega, but I will tell you a secret. I'm not really. I am a Beta's daughter. I was made an Omega so they could sell me. So you won't be diminished by me, Delta."

Beta's daughter! Roust gurgled suggestively to Easton, who ignored him, *Could be good for us!*

Maybe ask her what she did to get sold? Easton suggested sarcastically, although he guessed it could be practically nothing in Nico's court.

Roust contented himself by delicately licking Arielle's face. Sparks.

DON'T YOU DO THAT AGAIN, Easton roared.

Arielle sighed with happiness, snuggling the tousled fur and shifting the heavy robe she was wearing so she could press her bare body against him. "The Moon Goddess gave me an incredible gift when she sent me from Blood Moon - she sent me to you. Your Beta will understand - there is nothing more powerful than the will of the Goddess. Goddess doesn't make mistakes, as I'm sure your Alpha and Luna will learn with time. So where better to seal our bond than here, at the Shrine to the Moon Goddess?"

Easton couldn't stifle his laugh. *Wrong Shrine for that!* Maybe if you could get her close enough to the water, Luna Kyoko would drag her down herself. Roust yelped a little at the thought.

Arielle looked at Roust with concern at the garbled sound, but continued. "I thank the Goddess for every blessing. I'm not sure if you've ever seen one of these?"

She reached into a large wooden crate not far from where she knelt in the snow, shaking out a bit of straw packing, and turned back holding a fat, black and white snake about as long as her arm. It looked more like a legless lizard than a snake.

"Moonsnakes are a gift from the Goddess. We breed them in Blood Moon. They are beautiful, venomous, dangerous. Oddly, they absorb shifter gifts. With enough of them concentrating their power, you cannot shift at all."

It had an uneven pixelated cow-like pattern of black and white patches. The snake was not moving at all. It takes a lot to freeze a snake to death, but it certainly didn't seem to be leaping around with joy.

"The darker ones tend to prevent you from shifting to human, and the lighter ones prevent you from switching into wolf. Isn't that amazing?"

Roust was amazed. He was also having doubts about Arielle. She was into snakes. So into snakes that she brought a box of them on a first date. Could he be with a mate who was that into snakes? Her scent said yes but his personal preferences were not so sure. Was her wolf into snakes? Easton snickered. He now understood more about the creepy reptile resellers he had stumbled across in the Northward.

"Watch," Arielle said with a smile. She gestured the Lycan to her feet, and he obeyed, which Roust also found amazing. That guy was simply enormous. Arielle stood and moved to the box, pulling out a snake by its tail that was whiter, predominantly, than the one that hung limply in her arms. She handed it to the unwilling Lycan, and he immediately dissolved into Levi. She jerked her head towards a robe on the shrine railing for him to put on.

"See?" She pulled out a dozen snakes that he would guess were slightly on the darker side, and laid them out, tail to snoot to tail, in a rough circle around him.

Try now, Roust said with curiosity, observing the snake fence.

Can't shift, Easton answered. Although that far from meant he could not regain control. He was just waiting. Arielle quickly laid out a large adjacent circle of lighter snakes. They lay immobile over the snow in sluggish misery.

You're gonna bang her in the snow by the Shrine Pond in a snake circle? Easton commented, *Romantic.*

Oh, I don't think I am. Roust replied, wagging his tail as Arielle returned from her task and patted him on the head through a gap in the circle, holding the last snake draped over her arm.

"You join me here," she gestured to the gap, waving him into the lighter circle. Roust sat heavily for a moment, evaluating her.

You seem very determined, Roust said to Easton dismissively, standing and heading towards the gap in a quick run, *This is a people problem now. See you on the other side. Try not to get your dick bit off by a snake.*

Arielle laid down the last snake behind him, closing the loop, and Easton was forced into his own body. Being naked in the snow was not a first choice, but he could bear it for as long as this conversation was going to take.

He looked up and both Arielle and the Lycan gasped, and knelt.

"Wilder! Oh my Goddess, I knew it was you! I know you were the one. You did all this so we can be together? But what about Nico?"

"Beta!" The Lycan was full prostrate on the ground, just outside the circle.

Easton ran a hand over his chin, and got to his feet. He tried to leave the circle and found an invisible wall. He reached down to move a snake, but couldn't touch it due the burning shock on his skin. He tried to kick one out of the way, but his foot was deflected.

"Could you please hand me a robe?" He asked the Lycan, who looked up in confused alarm but nevertheless, obeyed. He noted that the *Lycan* could move a snake, as he handed the robe over. And Arielle had. Why couldn't he?

Arielle was looking at him in the soft moonsnake glow, reflecting the light back over the snow.

"You're not Wilder."

"I am not. He is my cousin. What is he to you?" *That is where that scent I could not place came from - she has something to do with Wilder. She has a wisp of his scent about her. Her neck is clean but he has some kind of claim to this one.*

That's revolting, Roust admitted, *But I could maybe share with Wilder?*

"Nothing," Arielle muttered, "He is nothing to me."

Easton wished for Luna. There was a deep web of lies here, he could tell. The mate bond, and the freaky snake cage, kept him from pitching her into the pond and calling on the only goddess he had any respect for to judge her words.

"Please, he never mentioned you- what is your name?"

"Easton. Glacier Moon Delta. You?"

Don't tell her my name.

"It doesn't matter. My name is anything you want. You're here and I'm here and all you need to do is touch me and make me yours."

"Nope," Easton said with conviction, "Sounds like I'm not *yours* after all."

There were pawsteps in the snow.

Chapter 23 – Lycan Revealed

"Alpha," Easton called over to me, Ash a fiery light between the trees. She cantered a few paces, melting holes in the snow as she walked. She stopped, and gave him a nod. With a shriek of alarm that made Easton collapse, Arielle reached through the circle for a dark snake, creating a gap as she threw it into Easton's hands. He rolled into Roust, and back into the darker ring. Arielle picked up a white snake, and hid it in her sleeve. She motioned the Lycan, now Levi, into a place near her in the white circle.

"It means so much to have my new Alpha and her Betas and Gamma here to celebrate my marking with the Delta." She said evenly, stepping towards Roust through the gap in the circle. She put a hand on his head, "Our bond is truly blessed."

"The hell is all this," I demand, Ash giving me back control. I grabbed a robe off the shrine rail, shrugging into it as I move towards....dead lizards? Like. A lot of dead lizards...glowing dully.

Thoughts? I poll the group. There's enough wolfsbane in his system that Easton is still blocked from the mindlink.

Snake witch? Cole purses his lips.

Gamma frowns. *I was raised in a Lunar Rites family and this is not a ritual I know.*

Only Brooke is silent. I'm guessing Persia is having it out with Roust. Just to provoke her, Roust licks Arielle's hand, and Brooke pulls hers back as if stung. Ash and Falcon both growl.

"Don't touch them," Brooke warns as I reach for a snake, "They may burn you."

Well, Ok, Roust must have told her that. I guess he's not completely useless. Terrifyingly, the effect they have *is* a burning sensation, but they also put out my flame. I light up again, and the closer I get, my whole body and finally even my hands are snuffed out.

"Levi," I ask, "What are these?"

"I am so sorry," Arielle responds, cowering, "These are proprietary to Blood Moon. Omegas such as ourselves are not privy to their secrets."

"Yes, but you aren't really an Omega. And I didn't ask *you* anything."

Did I tell you her wolf's name? Ash sighs.

No?

It's Jem.

Explains why she's so outrageous, I agree.

Levi steps away from the circles of snakes, backing away towards the pond where Beta and Gamma are cornering him.

"I asked you what you knew about these things, Levi?" I repeated.

Brookey and I clutched each other in surprise. Instead of shifting into his Lycan, Levi suddenly manifested huge bird-like wings, and launched himself into the sky.

"Look at that," Brooke said breathlessly.

"I know." I whispered back. I could not look away.

"You two gonna be ok?" Cole said irritably, leaning on his stave in the incandescence of moonsnakes.

"Mmmhmm." Brooke answered with distraction. Roust growled; she ignored him.

"Nice, Beta." Cole said dismissively, although he also didn't look away.

"Alpha's orders," she whispered.

Grant snickered, "Air is thin up there, and freezing. So, he's headed back down aaaany second..."

We all ignore Arielle, who is petting Roust possessively, showing occasional flashes of her complete lack of clothes beneath her robe. We are all nude under robes right now, but we at least *started* with clothes. It's apparent from the way she rubs against him to get Roust's attention every chance she gets, her choice of apparel is purposeful.

"Can you...*Alpha*...that guy?" Brooke asked, still searching the treetops for Levi.

"Currently? Yes. He's still an Omega." But after I free him....

There's a crash, an *OOF* noise in the darkness accompanied by the breaking of branches, and the two Betas take off to collect our Angel wolfy. I look Arielle and Roust up and down dismissively before approaching the snakes again, and again I am extinguished. There is a flash of smirk from Arielle.

Levi reappears, his turn to be naked, arms and wings draped over a stave being carried between the Betas.

"YOU WILL NOT MOVE."

Brooke sidles sideways to put his dropped robe back on him, now that he is standing still like a statue, head down. Cole takes it from her.

"You enjoy this too much," he says to his sister. Brooke blinks. I swear, Lycans are always trouble. Even my mate wants to touch him.

"THE OMEGA WILL DO IT." I am not sure that my Alpha voice will work, with Arielle behind a wall of moonsnakes, but to my delight, she is compelled to comply. Resisting every step, she opens a gap in the chain, studiously closing it behind her to keep Roust trapped. I am so thankful that she is still under the auspices of the Omega caste. With distaste, she dresses the Lycan and closes the buttons in front, then steps back with hands folded.

"EXPLAIN THESE."

"Moonsnakes, Alpha." Levi whispers, "Created by the Moon Goddess and gifted to the Alpha of Blood Moon. They block shifter powers."

"Thank you," I say in my normal voice. Levi looks surprised, and terrified.

"HAVE A SEAT IN THE SHRINE." He hurries to comply. Worry flits across Arielle's face, just for a second.

"Alpha," She calls to me. I don't know why my title in her mouth sounds so profane. Everyone in Glacier Moon calls me Alpha. My mate calls me Alpha. The moms of my daughter's friends call me Alpha. But when she says it, it's almost an insult. Ash is dying to nip some respect into her, but the Omega is just outside a circle of moonsnakes and I don't know what that would do to a firewolf. You'd think the fact that she is bound to the Alpha Voice would be enough to get a touch of courtesy.

"Did he walk into that cage voluntarily?" I ask her.

"Of course, Alpha. He is my fated mate. We are destined to be together, always."

"Uh-huh, and how do you feel about that, Roust?"

"I can't shift in here, Alpha," he replies.

"That is my preference," Arielle says quickly. "I have found that wolves are more honest than men."

I want to disagree, with Roust as my primary evidence, Ash notes to me, *But I feel like I can't.*

"Respectfully, let his actions speak for him." Arielle is a determined one. She composes herself, smoothing her cloak and draping it around her evenly. She takes a step and a pause, step and pause, walking towards Roust in bridal fashion.

Brooke spun backwards, facing Grant. He put his hands out on her shoulders, "Steady, Beta."

I gave Brooke a sideways look, "You *will* turn forward, Beta."

Please don't make me watch them mark each other.

I ignored her plea, "*TURN, BETA.*" With a sharp intake that I knew betrayed a sob, Brookey obeyed.

"Into the pool," I nudge my head at Cole, and in two moves he staves Arielle into the water behind her. Roust hurls himself against the invisible barrier delineated by moonsnakes.

"You will ask the questions," I tell Brookey flatly. Arielle is bobbing in the shrine pond, treading water and whimpering. My mother looms in dark tendrils of mist at the waters edge.

Roust is pacing at the edge of his moonsnake cage, roaring and growling.

"*I-*" She hesitates.

"WITH SPEED, BETA." I prompt. I'm not going to let her take the easy way and just let Arielle die of hypothermia. Brooke is *going* to choose. Either *she* releases her claim on

Easton or she is going to subdue him herself. I'm done with these others dictating the path - *I* hold the leads, here.

"Arielle of Blood Moon," Brooke starts shakily, "Do you have a connection to Delta Easton of Glacier Moon?

"I do!" She howls, as my mother nods behind her, "He is my fated mate! Let me out of here!" Cole looms over her, holding the stave threateningly.

Brooke looks at me with desperation. She doesn't know what else to ask. She was raised in a Lunar Rites household and the idea of Fated Mate holds a lot of sway with her, even now.

"NEXT QUESTION, BETA." I am not letting her off the hook. "Try to think like *him*," I suggest, gesturing to Roust.

"Do you love him?" She almost whispers.

"I will follow where he leads and devote myself to pleasing him in every way!" My mother's expression behind her is a masterpiece. She nods to indicate that Arielle's words are truthful, but clearly she thinks little of her definition of love. Arielle is starting to look a bit blue.

"What do you think of a grown man who makes promises to a *teenager* and then betrays her when it's convenient?" Brooke asks. Cole and I exchange glances behind her back.

"Beta, I had no choice," Arielle misheard the question, "Alpha would have killed me if I didn't go with him. I didn't know Beta Wilder was Delta's cousin!"

"Would you say that a man who would spend the better part of three *years* leading a woman on is coldly calculating, or would you call him a lazy man who lacked anything better to do with his time?"

Roust blanched a little.

"Please," Arielle pleads, "Easton, Roust, please help me. I am so cold. I just want to be with you, I don't care about anything but you. I am dying! PLEASE!"

Only Brooke and I look to my mother for the truth of these words.

"Please pull her out, Alpha."

I nod to Cole; he fishes her out. Grant gives her a dry robe. Brooke takes her by the hand.

"Please," Arielle begs again, gasping, "I am just an Omega, a handmaid of the Goddess."

My mother rolls her eyes, dissolving back into the dark pool with a swirl.

Brooke leads her to the circle around Roust. He snaps at his wife, head lowered, ears flattened, growling. Brooke nudges a half frozen snake aside with her boot, and glides Arielle into the space. The Omega shifts into an unremarkable gray wolf. Roust leaps on her immediately, covering her in his furry warmth, desperate to protect her, yelping with strangled delight.

Brooke falls to her knees just outside the circle, hands flat in the snow in front of her.

"I release you. May moonlight be thy beacon," she said with a bow of her head to the snow, gritting her teeth through the pain Roust is causing with his nuzzles, before Persia took control and she was a copper blur through the trees.

"It's done," through heartbreak, through betrayal, I am still Alpha. I gave her the choice, and now we live with it. But I won't call her back for this part. Gamma asks for permission to go after her, which I deny. Give her a *minute* and let us finish this first. Beside me, Cole's sigh of irritation is soul deep as he looks away towards the dark forest. My only wish is for his steadying hand on my waist, right now. I was never supposed to be Alpha. But I *am*.

"Delta, you may claim your mate." I said, loudly to be heard over the yelping and guttural mewling inside the circle, "We will assign you new quarters out of the Packhouse and welcome her to Glacier Moon."

"Respectfully, Alpha," Roust lingers at the break around his moonsnake circle, ducking his head in what passes for deference from Roust. The Gray female sits, half under his haunches, sniffing for the crux of his neck. "My mate prefers to be in the Packhouse."

"How would that work?" Cole asks him in exasperation.

"You ask her, she's your sister." Roust retorts, sitting up, nonchalantly licking a paw and wiping it behind his ear, pushing away the female.

"The girl is right next to you," Cole is not buying whatever game this is, "I know you can smell her. We can all smell her. Just mark her and be done with it."

"On that note," Roust pads through the gap, the female whines in shock. "No, thanks. Can you see me with a subservient female? Like for more than 15-20?"

He contorts back into Easton, reaching for a robe from the ground.

"I'm sorry, that is so demeaning to say. It has nothing to do with being an Omega - she's not really an Omega, anyway. But, you know I don't want anything of my cousin's, either." Easton noted, with a shiver, Arielle standing and staring in disbelief as she followed him. "A mate I could never trust? Do you think *she* can handle Roust? I've never had any conviction in Fated

Mates, and I just don't see how being a pawn for an indifferent goddess serves me *or* you, Alpha."

Behind us, my mother ripples the water in delighted amusement.

"*Subservient*? I was never raised to be subservient to anyone. That mangy canine I can certainly manage," Arielle growls in disbelief as Jem falls away. "You," she addresses me, "Release me from this Omega mark now, and I'll show you subservient!"

Beta and Gamma take one step forward, but Easton growls her down until she cowers.

"Beta didn't choose you this time, Delta." I say levelly.

"She didn't reject me, either." Easton answers, picking up Arielle's discarded robe and handing it back to her. "We're marked and mated; she still has to say the words to my face. And on that note," He jogged a few steps backwards, " With your leave, Alpha, I'd like to go-"

"Leave not granted," I said, still totally annoyed, "Delta, you get on your knees and reject that girl, if that is your intention."

He paused, "I'd like Beta to witness that, Alpha, so she never has to wonder."

I pursed my lips, evaluating him for a long moment in the moonlight.

"Put him in the pool," I directed to Cole, who immediately tripped Easton with the stave and kicked him into the water.

"This is FREEZING!" Easton bobbed to the surface. "This is not how I want to die, Alpha."

Like he has a choice, Ash noted derisively as I paced the edge of the pool.

"We'll see."

"*Babe....*Alpha...when did you last eat?" Cole mutters to me, exchanging looks with my mother, who has re-emerged, skeptical.

Ignoring that. He's right though, I am both pissed *and* hungry. It's their job to look after me properly and bring snacks. I'm giving everyone an F on their next staff review.

"*ARE YOU HIDING ANYTHING FROM ME, DELTA?*" I snarl towards the water. "Answer quickly, or these will be the last stars you see."

Chapter 24 – Moonsnake Showdown

He better start talking or die here in this water. I hope I don't run out of patience before he runs out of lies. He starts with throwing Cole under the bus.

"I was placed as a guard to Autumn's room at Delta Gabes, rather than the cells, Alpha." He screams out.

"WHAT?"

Cole has a sharp, guilty breath.

"You put him with our *children*?"

"I didn't know about the Lycan! She never would have found him otherwise! It was a great placement!"

"Please!" Easton manages to shiver, trying to ignore my mother, a dark shadow flickering in the light of my flames.

"You hurt my best friend," I turn attention back to him.

"That was never my intention."

"And what are your intentions now? Wait, you are addled, WHAT ARE YOUR INTENTIONS, NOW?"

"Please Alpha, I intend to go home to my wife. I just want to serve you, and her." He's not drowning, so I guess that was true.

"And do what with this?" I gesture to Arielle, freezing and defeated.

Easton shakes his head, "Free her to find her Chosen Mate, as I have marked mine."

MAKE HIM DO IT! Ash yells at me. And I would have, to end this whole ordeal, but I do think he's right. There's a third party in this relationship and it's Brooke. She might not stay with him, that's her right, but I do think it would be meaningful to know that he said the words of his own volition, rather than being ordered. Is he calculating? A bit. Lazy? More routine than lazy; he likes predictability. And frankly, these jobs are insane, who wouldn't want that in at least one part of their lives?

I nod to Cole and a shivering Easton rolls onto the ice shelf. While he warms, Cole and I collect snakes.

"Please, don't hurt her," Easton cries out weakly as we approach Arielle, sitting in a miserable heap in the center of a snake circle.

"LIKE I EVEN WOULD!" I snap, and they all cower.

"Almost done, Babe," Cole says in a coaxing whisper, looking up at me with head lowered, "He's not being stupid on purpose. We are gonna be home in just a few minutes, and you can have so many snacks. This is almost done."

NOTHING IS DONE. I scream into the mindlink. How many moonsnakes are there? It's gotta be dozens. Thankfully they aren't slithering away, and they glow slightly, but they are everywhere. Each one I touch burns my hand, not just because they are frozen. Every gift from the Moon Goddess masks a bitter poison. She really is a malicious sociopath.

Speaking of, Arielle has gotten her strength back, and I happen to look over as she shifts.

"NO. YOU WILL STAY THERE." I am exhausting myself with these Alpha orders and I am hungry and where is Brooke?

Beta, you are required.

No immediate answer, which is odd. She is upset, certainly, but she is strong, and I picked her because I have every faith in her.

Easton is back in the mindlink, waiting for her response as well.

"Let me go get-"

"She doesn't want to see you," I dismiss.

"I'll go," Grant volunteers, handing the Lycan over to Easton. Before he can leave, my mother bumps him with a tray from just over his shoulder.

"Alpha," my mother calls gently from the shrine, "Come eat something before you run all the way back to the Packhouse." I'm 23 but my mamma is still looking after me, and she threw together a wonderful offering of fish and rice and dried fruit. She knows my moods.

Cole takes a few bites. Still no word from Brooke.

"I'll run her up," he says, "I'm faster, no offense Grant, and she probably just ran a bit far. I'll meet you at the Packhouse." The only reason I let him go is that my mouth was full at the time. He snapped up another tidbit, shifting into Falcon and dashing off after Persia.

I think, my mother said to me, evaluating the group in front of her shrine, *That you better solve this mate problem now.*

She was not wrong. Now that I was less distracted by starvation, I saw what she saw. A Lycan of questionable control, a treacherous Omega, my addled Delta and my sweet but scholarly Gamma. Delta was a force unto himself, in his normal state, and I might need that. Time to restore equilibrium.

"Delta, if you wish to make your rejection, my mother and I are prepared to witness your intentions." I say pointedly, between bites of onigiri.

"*OMEGA ARIELLE OF BLOOD MOON, I DELTA EASTON OF GLACIER MOON REJECT YOU AND YOUR WOLF AS MY FATED MATE.*" He spits it out so fast it has clearly been rehearsed.

"You need blood or spit or fur or teeth or anything?" he asks earnestly.

"No Delta, that is sufficient. Thank you."

"Should I sign something?"

"*No*, you're good."

Arielle is wailing. Arielle is begging. Everyone is cold and tired and unmoved. I dust my hands, preparing to give her the order, but Easton shakes his head.

"Save your strength, Alpha." That's the Delta I depend on. He nods to my mother, who uncurls her slow, inscrutable catlike smile. She moves her hand, wrapping a rope of icy water around Arielle's arm.

"Some things are not for us, no matter our greatest wish." She says to Arielle, "Say the right words and be released to find a new happiness."

OR DIE HORRIBLY. Ash growls.

Arielle puts her head down. Easton kneels in the slush before her. He takes her hands, and I wonder if he is really going to let her reject him. Roust clearly wouldn't mind a plural marriage.

But Cole is right; Easton is dominant.

"Now." He nods forcefully. Arielle kicks a little. She says the words, and then he falls backwards into the snow, his grin illuminated in the moonlight. His relief is palpable to us all. Arielle cries quietly to herself and gets a pat on the shoulder from a Naiad as consolation.

I gleefully send the message to Cole. No answer.

"Can you get the Betas? Either of them?" I ask my mother, Easton, and Grant. Nothing. Brooke has a stronger connection to the mindlink than most, she should be easy to find.

Luna Violet? She cannot reach the Betas, either. With a huff, I reach out for my father.

Chapter 25 – Alpha Mason

My father is on a journey of self-knowledge. He will tell you that he loved being Alpha, and he was long-serving in the role. A 30 year reign is an achievement, and the Pack he turned over to me was generally self-sustaining. He made investments in technology and infrastructure that allowed Glacier Moon to move away from merely survival, and all I hope is to continue his legacy.

As Alpha, he favored heavy dark woods and draperies in his office. He wanted his staff in suits and sunglasses, hair slicked back. It was a whole look. Although of course they were tolerant of us as children, they were unsmiling, serious men. This was a direct contrast to my mother's freewheeling boho sensibilities, which he complained of as being messy and disorganized.

And now, he lives in the Southern village, which due to prevailing winds is actually the snowiest part of the territory, in a maximalist designer loft with his boyfriend. Tevin is a treasure, a former Omega who has embraced freedom, and who regales my father with spicy novellas and also runs the small Pack press. I loved my father as Alpha, I love the man he has become in retirement, but, honestly, where does he even get these Hawaiian shirts? Oh, I know, he gets them from our counterparts in Hawaii, Orchid Moon, because they send them to me as well.

He has the thermostat set to a billion, and he is in an undershirt and shorts, watering his jungle plants when we arrive. He has an actual cat, slinking around the leaves. Delta hates cats most of all, but is endeavoring to ignore it. We stowed Arielle and Levi and the disgusting box of snakes and then came all the way out here, because Brooke and Cole are still out of contact. The one thing that connects us all that cannot be disrupted by any sort of magic or mechanical means is the ice around us, and that is a special gift of my father.

"Oh, no little grandbaby or houseguest? Did she find her mate? She was so excited. It's a big deal for an Omega, you know." Tevin smiles at us. We all wince. I am getting an occasional zing across my mate mark, which I guess is Cole's way of communicating with me when he cannot otherwise. I keep my fingertips over the place.

"Complicated," my dad tells him. He must have spoken with my mother, and not updated Tevin yet.

"Oh," Tevin recovers, "I'm sorry. I'm sure I'll hear the details later. What's this errand for today?"

Once he realizes that we are asking my father to go outside and sift the ice network for clues, Tevin immediately frets about outerwear. He is frantically going through a box in the closet.

"I can't find two matching gloves!" He complains. "Does this parka still fit you? I knew I should have ordered new wool socks - we shrank the last ones in the wash! Your boots are in a *state*."

"I think I'll just shift, my dear," my father says mildly. Tevin stares at him.

"In front of the children?" He looks back at us, "I mean, the Alpha?"

We are all fully clothed again, but anticipating shifting ourselves. Nudity is just not a big deal, when outdoors here. Most houses and bus stops and park benches have a storage for robes or blankets or at least towels. By far the most popular and ubiquitous fashion item in Glacier Moon is a knee length hooded robe lined with fur. Knee length on an average male - on me they usually touch the ground or I pick up a child's size.

Indoors, the conventions are totally different. Shifter wolves are huge and prone to roughhousing. Homes comfortable for people are often not built to contain that energy, or unruly tails. So shifting indoors is less common; naked bodies indoors are provocative.

"I'll step behind the lattice," my father assures Tevin.

"It's freezing!" Tevin sputters. He was a small wolf, and the cold affected him more.

My father offers reassurances, but we go outside to wait. Apparently, it's less concerning to Tevin if *we* are cold. Although, we are well fed and in good condition; we are not cold.

In a moment, Blaze steps out from behind a wooden divider. I haven't seen my father's wolf in years. Despite her name, Ash is a white wolf, common in the tundra, although as far as we know she is the only one with a coat of flame. And despite his name, Blaze is a large black wolf with blue eyes.

I did indulge in hugging him, hanging on for a moment the way that I used to, the way that Autumn still hugs Falcon and any other wolf she can sneak close enough to surprise. She hasn't ever been able to hug Ash, due to the fire that surrounds her as soon as I shift.

Blaze turns in the snowbank, rolling out a flat place. He lays with eyes closed for a long moment, sensing the ice stretching out beneath him for miles in all directions. He twitches his ears. Delta, Gamma and I are ready to launch in any direction.

"Beta Brooke...." he mutters, "Persia is coming back this way. Alone. Slowed by injury. She should be close enough to link, now."

Delta interprets my side eye as permission and Roust is off like a shot. Another shock across my neck as we wait for an update from Blaze.

"Beta Cole....*not* Falcon...is just outside the territory border with....mmmmm...."

"What?"

"Did you say you picked up a Lycan with the girl you brought me?"

"Yes, and dad, he's a *nuisance*," That word is doing a lot of work for me here, "but he's still an Omega for now."

"Well, I think you have some royalty planning a visit. It may be a coincidence."

"*Is Cole ok?*"

"Beta is ok," Blaze nods, "But he is not at liberty to return, I think."

"*WHAT?*" Oh, my mate was kidnapped. By Lycans. Outside the territory.

Ohhhhhhhhhhhhhhhhhhhhhhhhhhhhhhhhh no. Ash is jabbering and as much as I love her, I push her down a bit. I need to think!

Back in 30, Delta chimes in, *Not that far but slow going.*

"Should I go carry her back?" Gamma asks me.

Blaze shakes his head, glancing at me. "She is ok. I think you are going to need that time to plan."

Chapter 26 – The Heartline

Kylie and Cole Flashback

It seemed like another item of clothing came off every time we got alone together. I had been coming to the Delta apartment to watch TV after school or on weekends for years, but now I was 'watching TV' from behind Cole's locked door, with one ear open for Gabe. Brooke was involved in *every* after school activity, and Gabe was intensely busy. There was less supervision than normal, but a lot more stress, particularly in the Alpha quarters.

All the adults were busy this fall, preparing for the spring ceremony and the change in government. Whatever was going on with my dad and mom, my high strung older sister and the mousey biographer who was constantly tailing them, it was *better* with Cole. He, like his father, was not easily ruffled. Cole and Brooke didn't have screaming matches over who borrowed and ruined new shoes or tracked mud into the office or how dignitaries were accidentally made to wait an embarrassing amount of time. Brooke might bounce a soccer ball off her brother's head and then they might roughhouse around the living room, but it was instantly forgotten the minute either of them recalled the existence of snacks. Between the *abundant* snacks, the relative peace, and the warm, cozy body snuggled next to mine, Delta apartment was a gift.

WE WERE ON COLE'S BED, not doing anything other than watching October snow fall in the endless twilight outside. He had his arms wrapped around me.

"Hey," he said softly, "Would you be willing to try something?"

"What?"

"I've already told you, your smell is delicious. It drives me crazy."

"You're crazy, that's detergent. You can't really scent me until 21, everyone knows that."

"Sure, but there is a scent to you that just comes off in waves. I love it. I love when you return my jackets and they smell like you." He slid me into his hoodies, and handed off his flannel without hesitation.

"You want some more of my soap?" I was not following.

Cole sat up with me, "The closer the clothes to your warm skin, I've noticed, the stronger the scent and the longer it lasts."

"Ok?"

"So. Can I put you in one of my t-shirts?"

"Right now?"

"Yeah. Then I can-"

"What?" I asked with an eyebrow.

"Wear it. Keep you close to me. Think of you, in *terrible* calculus."

"Ok." I answered, scooting back a bit. Cole kissed me impatiently. Perhaps my scent was on my lips as well? He slid my long sleeve shirt up over my head, rubbing hands down my arms before crossing his hands across his own body to get *his* shirt off. He held his chest against mine, pulling me up on my knees, arranged between his own. He flicked open the button of my jeans, and slid them down my thighs to the bed, leaning me over backwards to quickly work them down my legs and off, before helping me up again. I giggled, arms around his shoulders. He huffed into my neck, nibbling at the place where fated mates marked each other. Then he pulled his gray cotton t-shirt down over my head and arms, and smoothed it into place.

"Thank you." He adjusted his legs so he could lay back again, and pull me down with him. He closed his eyes, listening to our breathe and his music on the stereo.

Only for a moment. I carefully swung my knees to either side, sitting up to straddle him across his naked waist. I traced my name with a finger across his chest.

"Comfy," he asked, with a slight groan.

"I thought you said," I drawled, "It was better if I was warmer." I leaned forward to kiss him on the chin, "So warm me up."

"Ky," he said, through the kiss.

"Yeah?"

"I really love you," He said, moving hands in parallel up my thighs and under the hem of the shirt, "And you are never leaving me for some other Pack Alpha."

"How are you going to stop that? There's envoys here every week to get a look at Ellie, and they take notes on Violet and me as well."

"I'll mark you," he nipped me.

"Ouch! What if I'm not your Fated Mate?"

"Who cares?!"

I didn't answer. He stopped kissing my neck, flipping me underneath him.

"I said," he repeated, "I love you."

I didn't answer, looking away. How could he understand how much I want him? The comfort of him? The touch of him? But I had to hold myself apart, as Alpha's daughter.

"I love you, Kylie."

I flicked my eyes at him. He sat back.

"You don't love me?" He said with an incorrigible smirk.

"Of course I love you, you *absurd* wolfy Cole!" I finally burst out.

He snickered, working his way down from my chin. He stopped at my navel and looked up again.

"Ky."

"Mmm?"

"Promise you won't tell Brookey about this?"

"About what?"

He kissed my hip.

"She's one of my best friends!"

"You can't date both of us!"

"I'm dating you; she's my friend. Friends discuss stuff."

"I have to deal with enough awkward dinner conversations as it is."

"So don't tell her what? You're obsessed with my detergent and *OH MY GODDESS COLE YES-*"

Chapter 27 – Cole Captive

In the Outlands

"It's usually Rogue children we stumble across in the dark wood," observes the Lycan male.

Cole groaned against his bonds.

"I like the look of this one," the female purrs.

The male does a quick blink, "Of course you do - when's the last time you came across a *Beta* out delivering treats to granny?"

"A red one, at that?" The female drawled, "Still, it's a shame the other got away."

"She smelled Beta as well. Which is odd. Glacier Moon has a reputation for being odd."

"Maybe a family of Betas? They looked alike."

"Well. No matter. How's that bark taste, Little Red?" the male snickers. Cole's arms are wrapped around a tree, tied securely. The silver torc is the thing giving him the most trouble. It prevents him from shifting and burns besides. It slides over the mate mark on his shoulder and he flinches at the jolt.

"How old are you, Beta?" the female asks, with a turn of her head.

"Why does that matter? He's old enough to be Beta, so he's at least 21. Glacier Moon's Alpha came of age very recently, I think."

"I have standards," the female touches her long dark nails to her chest, looking Cole over.

"Shall I check his teeth for you?" The male raises a doubtful eyebrow at the cloth stuffed in Cole's mouth. He may not be able to go full fang due to the torc, but even shifter *people* were plenty bitey.

"No. No, we will assume he's better than an Omega."

"He does complicate things, a bit."

"Not for me, he's exactly what I came for. More than one would be nice - some of the traditional Packs offer us multiple tributes, which is very classy, but he's particularly well suited I think. A pleasant change from the house slaves they are always pawning off on us. Those hardly last a minute. It will be a while before I can wear *him* out."

"Well, if you hadn't lost the little female I would also be satisfied with our takings, but as it is, I am still without a tribute, and since we did come all this way, and Glacier Moon does owe us, I would like to have the full benefit of our advantage."

"Well, march on down there and take your pick."

"Are you sure Glacier Moon hasn't already been bled of tributes?"

"Quite sure, why?" The female ran a long finger down the back of Cole's neck, over his shoulder, and traced his spine. He had a large linear tattoo of a falcon with flame wings across his back, which she admired. "This is quite well done." Cole ground his teeth on the rag.

"I scent so few Omegas."

"Hm," The female delicately sniffed the air. "He smells amazing," she commented. "Buttery, salty, a complexity of vanilla. Bright smooth summer berry, but a tantalizing wisp of wood smoke. Complex. The perfect mix of savory and sweet. Exactly what I like."

She snapped her teeth in Cole's ear, and then stepped back. "I do generally prefer never asking for permission, particularly from lesser wolves. What is their Alpha going to do if we just collect a few Omegas anyway? It's really a favor, and they know it's our right. I suppose we could send an announcement to the Alpha? Informing them of our request? Then they can just have them ready for pick-up."

"He's marked," the male pointed out, "So both Alpha *and* his mate will probably offer you a lesser trade."

She made a face, "No, I like this one. Moon Goddess knows what she did to us, and what she owes us. Even if they offered me multiples, I still want this one. He's got the scent of experience, and I like the look of his hands. I hate breaking them in every time."

"He big enough? To get it where you need it?"

"Seems ok," she shrugged, looking Cole over, "Good size."

Cole took a calming breath.

The male considered, "There might be something to that. You must be doing it wrong, all these years and still no pups."

With a squeal of artificial rage, the female contorted into a huge beast, and chased the male out of the grove. Cole closed his eyes, ignoring their playful growling in the trees around him, trying again to free his hands. The mindlink was useless off Pack territory. Once he scented Persia, not even that far from the Packhouse, he found her retreating backward while growling at a hidden threat. These two grabbed them up, rolled them in sacking, and dragged them over the snow for ... who knows. It would have been bad enough in wolf form, but as a human it was all he could do to protect his skull from being slammed into rocks and trying not to roll over, to keep his face from being scraped off. Brooke had not been conscious, with a clearly broken arm, when they turned her out on the other side of the border, dozens of miles from the Central Packhouse and even the Southern villages. But she also was no longer wearing the silver torc - it had cracked in the cold and the repeated blunt hammering as they careened over the ground. Persia recovered before Brooke, shifted and bolted like a slippery salmon before the Lycans could react.

They could easily have overtaken her, and gave chase for a minute or two, but really couldn't much bother with a broken one, anyway. Now they regretted it. A matched pair of Beta breeders would have been a distinction among all the sullen and sallow Omegas that were normally procured for this purpose. Widmer and Widra were stunning to look at, lucky to have found each other in a relatively short amount of time, as conceited in their arresting physical attributes as they were complacent in their strength and power. Their relationship was passionate and intense, *dramatic*, but after decades, not procreative. This was the one chip in their smooth, gleaming surface, a known trait common in Lycan lines. She loaded her precious treasured Lycans with gifts, but Moon Goddess ensured their rarity.

"How do we start?" Widra mused, fetching a scrap of paper from her pack. She idly leaned against the tree that currently kept Cole immobile, studying the paper and occasionally indulging in a twirl of Cole's red curls behind his ears. He flinched away, which *delighted* her. Their pups would be beautiful, and even more rare in color.

"Dear Alpha," Widmer suggested, "Per the ancient agreement...no....under the authority of the ancient agreement... of your people with the King of the Lycans, we hereby request...."

"No, it needs to be more direct, powerful. *Threatening*."

"We hereby provide notice that we will be arriving in ...12 hours time?"

"Sure."

"To receive the customary offering of...six? Six Omega tributes."

"What else do they have at Glacier Moon?"

"Ask your boyfriend."

"*Mwher*, cutie, what is it that Glacier Moon normally provides the Lycan King on tribute years." She snagged the rag out of his mouth with her nail.

"You ulcerated horse-faced bitch, you better let me off this tree right now. There is not shit for you coming from Glacier Moon, except a lesson that is going to rub your moron smiles right off your goddamn dirty mongrel muzzles."

"Oooo, lucky I don't need your dirty mouth for anything." Widra giggled, quite used to resistance from the lesser beings. Cole bared his teeth.

"His teeth are quite good, Widdy."

"*Fuck. You.*"

"What a jackpot you've found," Widmer answered, still working on the written request. "Pity you couldn't hold on to *mine*. He'll be all out of that defiance in a few hours."

"He's a Beta, not a half dead Omega." She replaced the rag with a stick in his mouth, "Adorable. You look like a puppy bringing a present home to mama."

"They all have limits. He'll be kneeling soon enough."

Historically, Lycan kings might indeed have some kind of archaic contract for so many Omega breeders and so many wheels of cheese or jars of honey or cords of cedar shingles, or whatever, to be made available once every set number of years, for each Pack in their territory. Kylie already had a deal with the Lycan King to end this practice, which she negotiated when the last Lycan Omega showed up and Glacier Moon was swarmed with hyper-aroused suitors aplenty. But apparently Widmer and Widra weren't privy to the most updated Annotated Code. Or they were lazy and just thought they could get away with a raid.

BACK TO ALPHA

I sat on the warmed bathroom tile, back against the wall, boots crossed before me and tucked under one of the many looming potted plants. It was sweltering in the bathroom, despite being well below zero outdoors. I held a folded towel in my lap, and dad's creepy cat keeps popping out from behind the monstera leaves to eyeball it. Invitation to sit in my lap is not offered, and she is offended.

Brooke was curled in the tub beside me, head laid tiredly on the tub rail. Her red braid hung down and made a puddle, evaporating quickly on the heated tile. She was warming up and healing, explaining how she stumbled into the Lycans. Since it was his bathroom, Dad also invited himself into the small space, and he was perched on the sink, arms crossed. Tevin, Easton, and Grant lingered in various fashion in the hallway outside the cracked door.

Easton clapped his hands together and snapped his fingers intermittently as he paced. Tevin already made him a tea and offered him a beer and still the man would not sit. He told me he had gotten about 20% of his brain function back in one glorious rush when he finally divested himself of Arielle, and another good bit when Roust ran out to Persia and the two of them made their careful way back to the Old Alpha's apartments. It was such an improvement over the hazy sluggishness he struggled under for the past few days that he was frenetic and ready to go, ready to run anywhere, shred anything. No, Brooke hadn't offered him acquittal, yet. But she was currently slightly brain damaged, so once Persia healed her, he was sure full forgiveness was forthcoming.

No comment.

The question, for me, was not what to do next. Anything invading my territory and snatching my people violated all boundary agreements and I am well within my rights to exact whatever justice I deemed appropriate, *even* outside my borders. *Even* if these idiots *hadn't* laid hands on *my mate* and *Beta*. The issue was that Persia was quite insistent that she wanted to join. Apparently Widmer needed some lessons about keeping his hands to himself. But Brooke was not ready. Her arm would mend, but it would be days, and she had a skull fracture.

"It's minor," Persia told Ash, who told me. "If she stays shifted, I can manage."

"Where are the moonsnakes when you need them." I muttered.

"Moonsnakes?" Dad asked from where he was holding court on the sink. I gestured my father out of the room, giving Brooke a hand up and the towel.

"You wanna come to this party?"

"Yes, Alpha." She is quiet.

"Mason, she can just stay here. I really don't think-" Tevin filled the doorway with disapproval.

"Alphas call." Dad offered a conciliatory smile. I know he takes pride in me, as a daughter and Alpha. He provides a sounding board but rarely steps in. He was grateful that I accepted the Alpha role, and he was freed to remake his life with Tevin. Knocking heads is not his interest anymore, although he is genuinely concerned about Cole.

"You will stay shifted; You will defer to Persia." I ran a litany of regulations over Brooke, making eye contact with Easton and Grant.

"She's great, she's gonna be fine." Easton said with assurance, pacing.

"Well dry her hair, at least!" Tevin answered with exasperation.

My dad laughed. "I think Persia better take over. Outdoors. Tevin, close the door so the cat doesn't get out right now, please, hon."

In the yard, preparing to head to the border, I do a quick check in with Luna.

Did you find them? She asks in response.

Working on it. We retrieved Persia and I'm about to get Falcon. Sometimes, when I know I would tear up or get emotional talking about him, it's easier to refer to his wolf.

Ok sweetie, I'm sure he's gonna be just fine. He's so strong.

Me too. I know he is. I also know what the Lycans want of him.

Do you want Olivia or Joshi? For backup?

No, I have dad if needed. How are things there?

How do you think? She said sarcastically. *I hope you get Delta back to us in one piece because this Lycan is bonkers. He has no idea how to control his shifts. I had to put him in the rock cave!*

That's the oldest, worst cell. A legacy of a less progressive history, when Glacier Moon did have a dungeon packed with breakfast-making slaves.

I stuffed it full of those clove balls Cole made, and the big guy appears to be asleep. What did you do to him, that he has wings now? Is it the snakes?!

Don't kill him!

*Please, it would take more than a hit of catnip, to a Lycan. But I just want to point out, the work you do is important, of course, **Alpha** Kylie, but **I** am the one addressing all the concerns here. And it's a lot. You could clue me in a little more. I don't necessarily want to use the word 'skank,' but this girl Arielle is also causing-*

Def don't want to hear any more about her today, Ash mutters to me.

Don't let her near the moonsnakes! Couldn't do it without you, Luna. You have my full faith.

Call me if you need me. She answers dryly, *Good luck.*

Chapter 28 – Invaders

"Oh good, you brought her back. We don't even need this invitation now." Widmer throws the paper into a ball over his shoulder.

"Will you look at that one?" Widra turns towards the Pack. Or, what she can see of the Pack, which is just me and Persia.

"Alpha," I walked over the tight-packed snow, carrying the stave, trying not to check my stride as I catch sight of Cole tied upright to a tree, forehead pressed against the wood. He doesn't move, but he must hear me.

"Alphaaaaa," she drawls in surprise, "Of Glacier Moon?"

I'm not gracing that with an answer. "I'll take my Beta back, thank you."

"Oh. *Alpha*! Female. I did not know that; congratulations on your accession. We were just putting together an introduction, planning to present ourselves and accept our Omegas and other tributes."

"On behalf of the King," Widmer adds. "Widmer, and my mate Widra, your Alphaness."

"I know who you are. If Ted had any interest in you, he would have sent me a message himself."

"*Ted*, is it?"

"First name basis with the King?"

"We have an understanding." Even under the long cloak, I look small beside them. I look small beside Persia. "An understanding that Glacier Moon provides no tribute other than courteous hospitality. Certainly, no people."

"What were we saying earlier, Winny, about the major exports of Glacier Moon? Seems the major exports are discourtesy and disrespect to the ruling Lycans." He looks me up and down, running his tongue over his teeth. "We are *off* Pack lands, Princess *Alpha*. You have a fence and everything. It is miles away."

To the side, I can see Widra searching a bag, I'm guessing for a torc or two. She looks up, and narrows her eyes at Cole, and then examines the darkness. This one doesn't hunt or she would know for *sure* that a big, dark wolf is closing in on her. That's not Cole's scent, giving her pause. Roust is pressed down against the snow, a blurry shadow at the foot of a snowdrift. Her vision should be superior, but she is not a creature of instinct. Like a teacup poodle, instinct has been bred out of the upper class in favor of beauty for generations. Roust very much relies on raw instinct.

I wasn't necessarily meaning to crack my neck when I moved my head to the side, but it did work in the moment. "My lands are anywhere that my Pack is; you know that, Lycans."

Widmer takes in both me and Persia, addressing Widra in a self satisfied tone; "I don't object to just taking in the whole Pack then. I was already planning on sniffing out the redhead, and you at least have rudimentary style and amateur poise, so I think we can get along nicely. Along with Widra and *her* prize, of course."

"I have the collars, Widdy. We will turn all the heads, walking these three in the park, can you imagine?" Widra roamed a possessive hand between the tree and Cole's stomach, wrapping her fingers around his torso, sliding her face against his to put lips to his cheek with a low purr. I could see him try to pull away from her touch.

"We only want that which is ours." He gave a sudden, choked scream of surprise that almost dropped me, because the old bag shifted, dealing Cole a brutal rake across his waist as she retracted her arm.

She wasn't expecting Delta to leap on her shoulders and slash her face with manic savagery. And she wasn't expecting Gamma on the other side of the encampment, as he dashed forward and freed Cole. There was blood on the snow around them.

Widmer shifted as Widra did, but Persia had already gotten a good hold and thrashed open a rip before he was fully fur. He was distracted by Widra's cry of surprise as she grappled with Roust, and then Jabot as well, enough that Persia got in another bite and jerked her head to open another ragged gash on the Lycan.

I waited, just one second longer, long enough to see Cole roll clumsily into Falcon, shaking himself before launching into Widra.

Ash was more than ready to light up the night.

MINE! She bellowed, head down and ears flattened, in a mane of flame like a meteor, catching Widmer completely by surprise.

LUNA.

We stopped back at my dad's on the way back. He sent Tevin to his office and closed the door, because Persia and Falcon were still shifted and there was a nonzero chance that his plants or his cat would be altered by the experience. When we were kids, we would often come home to find wolves in various stages of recovery draped over the Alpha suite furniture, but Tevin is finding this very intrusive.

I am finding Falcon laying over *me* very intrusive, as well as warm, as I try to continue my conversation with Luna.

Still there? She asks.

Yeah, I push his huge furry head out of my lap, but he just circles like a dog and exchanges his head for his front paws. *I need you to send an urgent message.*

Got it. Email?

I guess, that's fastest. Ready? Dear Ted,

King Ted?

Dear King Ted, owing to some significant overstepping on their part, I hope that you will promptly find two of your nationals in the crevasse located at Sukakpak. While Glacier Moon remains your most committed partner, raids on citizens cannot be tolerated. I trust you will deal with Widmer and Widra appropriately.

Nice. I'm sending to all three of his assistants. They still alive?

They were when we kicked them in there. Falcon rolls over again, offering me a back leg and his fluffy red tail, more like a fox than a wolf. *Please also add that I am looking forward to seeing him at the Equinox celebration.* I open and close my hand with a wince. Ash could never burn me, but collecting those stupid silver torcs strewn over the snow did, across the same raw half-healed skin that was damaged by dozens of moon snakes. Ash is doing her best to speed that healing process. Luna signs off to send the message, and Falcon playfully licks my good hand. Cole is ok, but needs to recuperate a bit more. I give Falcon pets over his muzzle and ears.

On the other sofa, Easton sits with his head back, quiet for the first time in days. Persia is over his lap, asleep. Beta needs a bit of recovery as well, although possibly Brooke is malingering so she doesn't have to deal with her mate. Grant is passed out in the middle of the floor on a pile of throw pillows, with the cat curled on his back.

Chapter 29 – The Moon Goddess

"Someone here to see you," my mother nods shortly, gesturing me into the guesthouse where she has taken up residence. She has told me that she loved living in the Packhouse as Luna, with all the kids running around and the buoyant energy. But those last few years, between me, my siblings, and my father, were less joyful and she is valuing her peaceful space.

In the bright wood living room, there is Serena, one of the diminutives of the moon goddess herself, awash in a shimmering mass of silvery gray robes. She is not smiling.

"Ladyship?" I venture, trying hard to hide my annoyance.

Grant, can you bring me the tank of moonsnakes please? I'm in my mother's guesthouse.

Yes, Alpha. I asked him because he's the only one who wouldn't push back, or trip and drop the damn thing.

"You have something of ours, Alpha," Serena sneers at me.

"Yes, your snakes are on the way. Is there anything else?"

"Your charge is wreaking havoc at the convent of our sisters. Your lack of training and discipline have proved to be a disappointment, there."

"Well, I neither trained nor disciplined her. They can bring up their concerns with Blood Moon."

"You shall be respectful," the pale goddess intones. "Your lack of deference has not been unremarked. I will remind you that the Moon Goddess, the mother of all Shifters, is the source of all life and hope, and you do well to venerate her, lest she take back your gifts in the face of ingratitude." My mother, behind her, rolls her eyes.

"Respectfully, Ladyship, Glacier Moon has just endured a season of unnecessary chaos at the hand of your mistress. Neither Omega castes nor Fated Mates nor *Angel Wolves* are gifts that serve this Pack well. Beta Princess got rejected, so you connected her to his *mated* cousin here? *Lazy.*"

"You are the ones who seem to believe you have the entitlement to choose your mate. Moon Goddess observes no such claim."

"Well you can start with Alpha Nico over at Blood Moon, then. Speaking of, you will note that we took careful care of your pets."

"All gifts of the Goddess shall be properly revered and stewarded."

"Uh-huh, well here's the thing. These came from Blood Moon and I am going to need your express assurance that they will be destroyed and not returned to Alpha Nico or any of his associates."

The silence told me everything.

"Serena, I will not release them to you without your explicit promise."

"Have you not noticed?" Serena asks, eyeing Grant as he came in with a writhing tank of black and white snakes, "There are far fewer Omegas here than before?"

Grant is stricken dumb. He has less interaction experience with imperious deities than I have.

If you dare kneel, I will demote you. I warn him. I can see the weakness in his knees, begging to grovel.

"Yes, Ladyship, because I grant them a change in Aura. It takes hours of my week that I would like to devote elsewhere." I answer her calmly.

"Nonsense. Fewer Omegas are being *born* into Glacier Moon, since you abhor them so forcefully. It is not the fault of the Goddess that you take on Omegas from all the other territories."

"Frankly, I find it abhorrent that you would allow any creatures to exist as less than equals, and turn a blind eye to the insidious abuse in almost every Pack but this one." Less Omegas are being born, because once again, there are less Omegas, due to my policy. It has nothing to do with the Goddess. She has no interest in us. She is just knocking around her shrines, getting pissed off that nobody is lighting her incense or scraping the algae out of her moon pools. But moon snakes aren't negotiable.

"These will not make their way back to Blood Moon." I don't get my power from this goddess or the moon, I get my power from the water and the ice and the midnight sun. I light up my hands and the snakes respond to the warmth.

"As you wish, as you wish, Alpha! She has her reasons. The Omegas serve her, as do you all. At least, they know how to venerate their Goddess. You don't know how to mind your own people, before getting involved in the affairs of others. You *prefer* a messy, ill organized Pack and if *you* are struggling with management and authority, may I suggest you observe the scribed rituals of Moon Goddess worship for some practical advice."

"Oh, no thank you, we left the Middle Ages." And I don't *need* a class of citizens who are kept in a state of fear and pain so that *she* can have reliable worshippers and the Lycans can get dates.

"When is the last time you offered supplication in the shrine of the Goddess?"

I look sideways at my mother. She shrugs. I manage to suppress most of a laugh.

"Never. I have never done that. If you will excuse us, I am quite tightly scheduled. Here are your reptiles. I do hope you will keep a closer eye on them in the future, and I will leave you to continue your visit with my mother, who is, as you know, a Naiad, and in no way dependent on the Moon Goddess for any of her gifts."

"Tea, Serena?" My mother asks cheerfully. "You won't believe what my sassy little granddaughter has been up to recently, and I have the pictures to prove it!"

"No, thank you, Kyoko. I will leave you with your troublesome Alpha. Let us hope her daughter has more sense when she comes of age."

"I do hope so," I fervently pray, "Because in 13 more years I will be ready for a vacation."

"That's what I thought, too," my mother sighs, as Serena dissipates into motes of light. "I had to wait 18. Well, she's just as uptight as she has always been. You do have a way of getting under her skin. It's good for her. She needs her complacency rattled from time to time."

"I'm sorry to be rude, mom, but they really have no idea what life is like for shifters."

"Don't take it personally, dear," my mother pours a teacup for me and Grant, as well as herself.

"It sounded very personal," Grant notes.

"She's just mad about Levi. I think winged wolves are a relatively *new* thing they've chosen to bestow on their favorites, the Lycans, and it embarrassed them when their little princeling didn't make it, but it embarrassed them even *more* that he *survived* but he was turned Omega. So they had no *clue*."

"Because they don't give a shit about Omegas!"

"Because they don't give a shit about Omegas," my mother confirms with a nod.

Chapter 30 – Moonsnake Magic

It's been a few weeks. I am behind my desk at our regular morning check in. Luna shrugs her shoulders - we are waiting for Brooke and Easton, who are late.

Beta? This is a 9am meeting and it's 9:15. Delta, are you with her?

Um, she's here, Alpha. Please go ahead and get started. She's been off schedule since she got up.

You ok, Beta?

Great! She chirps brightly, *Be right there.*

"Ok, let's just get started. They are on their way." It's like one floor down, the Beta Suite. Honestly.

"They weren't at breakfast," Grant notes. Ok, maybe Brooke finally gave in and forgave him. It's been rocky with them, the last few weeks. There is a chorus of snickers and howls.

"Leave it, that would be a blessing. What else is on the docket?"

"Well, since Delta is not here, I'll start by saying that the Moon Sister's convent *notes* that they will not be accepting any more acolytes from us without a strict vetting process."

"Arielle is a pain in the ass, separate and distinct from being an Omega." I shrug. I am in no way sorry that I shipped her off to the convent. The pamphlets were still in the Delta suite from when Gabe threatened Brooke all those years ago, and they were very eager to reform a fallen woman.

"Heritage committee wants to meet."

"Please make that happen," I nod. Nobody knows how the Pack came here, how long ago or under what circumstances - the first shifters who ended up here were not known for their great literacy- but what is clear is that there are inhabitant groups that predate us, and that conversation with them is ongoing.

"Done," Violet nods.

"Don't tell her about the caribou. I want to tell her about the caribou!" Olivia says with a laugh.

"*What* about the caribou?"

"The *main herd* of caribou got stuck on the wrong side of the river when it started softening, and they are causing traffic and mud on the east flank and one of them bit a *mailman*!"

"A caribou? I thought it was *Moose* that bit-" Grant begins, with shining eyes.

"No, please." I put out my hand.

"You wanna go round them up?" Cole wags his eyebrows at me.

Oh my goddess yes. Don't you? Are caribou hunts below my dignity?

NO! Ash answers.

Who cares! Is Cole's response.

"STILL ENJOYING SOFA life?" I pop in to the Beta Suite, as these two never appeared. Easton is comfortably arranged on the sofa, where I know he has been sleeping for weeks.

"So many throw pillows," he nods, "And the big tv is out here."

"You ok? You missed the meeting that you *said* you were coming to."

"Brookey...is being slow." Easton drawled, nodding down the hall to the bedroom.

"So?" I didn't move. I'll talk to her in a minute. I'm not here for the dirty details if this was make-up sex morning; even with long-marrieds sometimes you still might miss breakfast. But you're not gonna *tell me* you are on your way and then not show.

"I am sorry, Alpha." He grovels a bit.

"You should be, I almost took you off the caribou hunt."

"Caribou hunt!" Roust flashes across his features.

"Yeah, herding with a side of hunt. Go get ready. I know you want to bring your puppy, Levi."

Easton grins with delight, but surprisingly, does not rush to obey. What is with these guys this morning? I go down the hall to the bedroom.

And there is a half put together Brookey, on her knees on the bed, clutching her pillow.

"What's wrong?"

"Every time I think I'm good, I just get another wave," she manages tearfully.

"Bad take-out or -?"

"I think I'm pregnant."

Him? I mouth as I gesture back down the hall.

"Of course him!" She answers in a rough whisper. "How did this happen!"

I blink at her. She looks up at my expression, and then rolls her eyes, "He's been sleeping on that sofa!"

"Didn't you tell me about a kinda ... "

Bad? Depressing? Unsatisfying? Ash offers me words.

"...*mediocre* encounter just after we were at Northwards?"

Her look tells me she knows.

"Well, congratulations!"

"What am I going to do?!"

"You're gonna have one to two fat little roly polies, and then you can dress them up for holiday cards in matching PJs."

So many things pass over her face.

"I mean, or not, let's be real, we live in modern times. You do have a choice. But I think you can handle this."

In answer, she falls over sideways.

"Stop," I say, "This is a good thing. This changes nothing. You still don't have to take him back. You will still be Beta. Everything is fine, Brookey, I promise. The morning sickness will pass, too."

She nods miserably.

"Oh! Well ok, one thing changes. You are not permitted on the Caribou Hunt today."

"There's a Caribou Hunt?!"

"It's gonna be a muddy slog through an icy river. I promise you will not miss any fun. We will bring you back a haunch."

"Oh goddess, please don't mention food. I'm really early, I could probably go?"

"Absolutely not," I said with a snicker, "You wouldn't let me go, when I was pregnant with Autumn. There will be more Caribous in the future. See? That's what you said to me at the time, and it was true!"

I pat her head, "Go get checked at the hospital, so we can plan better, ok? I'll miss you. But this is not a problem. We will hash out the details tomorrow."

Back in the living room, Easton is quickly tidying the sofa, folding the throw blanket and clicking off the TV.

"Congratulations." I nod to him. He grins back, but I am not smiling.

"I didn't want to leave her so sick," he attempts to explain.

"This is your lucky day," I tell him, "We depart in 90 minutes. I will go fetch your defective wingy-stringy Lycan. You go back there," I gestured over my shoulder, "And make this right with your wife, *right now*."

"Yes Alpha." He inclines his head.

"I REALLY WANTED TO go on the Caribou hunt," Autumn is sulking at dinner. The twins were put to bed early, but we let Autumn stay up for the Hunt Feast.

"Couple more years, honey," Cole promises, tiredly, "You have to be able to hold a stave, if you can't shift yet. They just run without looking where they are going."

"I do have a surprise for you after dinner." Missing a hunt is hard.

"Really? Is it a haunch?"

"No, I promised one to Aunt Beta and one went to the Lycan."

"Aunt Beta was sick allllll day."

"I know, she'll be fine."

Upstairs, Cole and I bring Autumn into the sitting area off our bedroom. It is dark, because everything is dark here all the time, but lit with a soft glow from a glass tank. I have a few moonsnakes in there.

"Snakes? Did you get me a pet?!"

"No sweetie, don't touch, these are venomous."

"They don't look very happy."

"They don't love the cold weather here, even with the heat on. But they have a mysterious magic. Watch."

I lit my fingers with their own warm glow of flame, but as I approached the tank, it was lighter and lighter and finally extinguished.

"Wow," Autumn says with concern.

"Now watch," Cole prompts, and I shift into Ash. Autumn has seen very little of her, to their equal unhappiness. Ash, flickering with fire, softly approaches the moonsnake cage, and in a moment, she is a beautiful huge white Arctic wolf, glowing but only in the reflected light of moonsnakes.

"Ash!!"

"Autumn! MINE MINE MINE!"

The two of them play and run and crash around the sitting room, Autumn clinging to her neck the way she has always wanted. Cole leans back against the dresser, merely observing and occasionally moving things out of the way to avert disaster.

After an hour, Ash is panting and it is bedtime.

"Can I have Ash in bed with me?" she begs her father.

"No, sweetie, the magic doesn't last forever. If she gets too far from the snakes, she will be fire again. She's special; we love that she's a fire wolf. This was just for tonight."

"She's wonderful! Mom is so lucky! The boys will be so jealous they missed it!"

"I know, we will give them a turn soon," Cole gives Ash some pets as well. He's never gotten to touch her before either. He leaves to tuck Autumn into her bed down the hall, but we don't shift. Because there is one other who has never gotten close to Ash. And that is Falcon.

I think I better get some water. Ash comments to me smugly, padding into the bathroom to find a drink. She's been waiting for him for a long time, and if she has it her way, they are missing breakfast.

Oh, it's going to be my way. We are the Alpha.

I was never supposed to be Alpha, but sometimes, things happen.

The door is pushed open softly, and Falcon comes in, fully arrested by the sight of Ash in the moonlight. Cole was right - we are fated mates. I can feel it, that draw like a magnet that I *never* fought against for one moment from the time I was fourteen, pulling across the room.

The End

Don't miss out!

Visit the website below and you can sign up to receive emails whenever E.L. Southwick publishes a new book. There's no charge and no obligation.

https://books2read.com/r/B-A-YMHDE-YCGRG

BOOKS 2 READ

Connecting independent readers to independent writers.

Also by E.L. Southwick

Absolute Unit
Lady Alpha
Firewolf

Watch for more at https://cindrebooks.blogspot.com/.

About the Author

E.L. Southwick's writing roots trace back over a century to small-town Connecticut and even further to the early colonists of Salem. Surrounded by stories from a young age, she found inspiration in romance and fantasy. Her work honors her family's legacy while incorporating modern feminist themes, focusing on strong, complex characters who reflect the struggles and triumphs of contemporary life.

Creativity and literature are the mirrors we hold up to inspire, and challenge societal norms. Through her writing, she aims to celebrate women's strength, spark dialogue, and build community among her readers.

Read more at https://cindrebooks.blogspot.com/.